T0128325

# Corky's Beach Bar

## PHIL PERKINS

authorHOUSE®

*AuthorHouse*™
*1663 Liberty Drive*
*Bloomington, IN 47403*
*www.authorhouse.com*
*Phone: 1 (800) 839-8640*

*Published by AuthorHouse  10/01/2019*

*ISBN: 978-1-7283-2963-5 (sc)*
*ISBN: 978-1-7283-2962-8 (e)*

*Library of Congress Control Number: 2019915340*

*Print information available on the last page.*

*Additional story ideas, character development and semi-true stories by Sandra Dube*

*Copy editing and cover art by Sandra Dube (wish she could just write the next book … I need a vacation).*

*This book is printed on acid-free paper.*

# Contents

# Dedications

This book is for a wonderful bunch of people from all over North America.

For my love and life, Sandi, my brother Randy (songwriter and musician), sister Bethany (noted author), my talented brother in law Peter, the real Gabe, sister in law Elizabeth (art gallery owner to the stars), our west coast family, Coco, Dennis (San Francisco bay area congas), Jeff, Chrissy, Dustin and Dave. Our island pals, Mark, Brittany, Beth, Taline, Sara, the real Duke (everything irie), Ryan, Kim, MaryBeth and Peter. To my buddy the first Andy, Taco (CLT), Pierre (RIP), to my bandmates (go Libra Sun!), John (Johnny Rocket), Mark (Dr. X), Peter (Peter Gunn) and Tom (Tommy Gunn) ...you guys rock.

Also, Corky C. and Mike as always for surf cred.

Much love to all,

Phil

# Prologue

"It's a semi-true story
Believe it or not
I made up a few things
And there's some I forgot
But the life and the telling
Are both real to me
And they all run together
And turn out to be
A semi-true story"
**Jimmy Buffett**

# From Our Last Episode (the book *"The Legend of Corky Sandoval"*)

Surfer Corky Sandoval and several friends were camped out in Daytona Beach for the winter. Corky and his friend Ken "Duke" Phillips had managed to surf up and down the east coast, even winning some minor competitions along the way. Duke was a Florida boy born and bred while Corky was raised in Hawaii after being born in Southern California. The two competitive surfers had always intended to move on when the weather improved on the east coast, but now both had jobs and at least some level of responsibility. Corky had landed an assistant manager job at a surf shop in Daytona called Jack's Surf and Sail, even though the owner's name was actually Andy. Long story.

Corky and Andy had become fast friends and, in part due to Corky's wins in the state of Florida, had decided to custom make surfboards with the brand "CorkBoards ™". Corky knew nothing about designing and building surfboards, of course, but Andy "knew a guy" as they say. Corky was simply the brand, although he did try out each line of boards so that he was comfortable lending his name to the final product. Business was good.

Duke on the other hand settled down for the Christmas rush working in his father's furniture store in Ormond

Beach, just north of Daytona. He had vowed not to do that but needed the money to help fund plans he, Corky and the others had formulated.

The "others" included Kaapo, a Hawaiian native and long-time friend and traveling companion who had known Corky since high school. Kaapo preferred to be called Gabe since it was the Finnish root to his Hawaiian name. Gabe fancied himself a photographer and based upon some of the work his companions had seen, he seemed to be on the right track. There was also Abby Colter whom Corky and Gabe had met in Half Moon Bay, California. Abby had worked in a greasy spoon they had visited upon arrival and hit it off immediately. Abby was a writer at heart and had a stated goal of traveling as much of the United States as possible looking for stories to tell. She was also a vegetarian with very particular eating habits. It was hard to tempt her with a burger as the group found out traveling together.

Then there were Alexa and Stacy, two girls from New England with a love of surfing and a healthy disdain for any guy who thought they couldn't be just as competitive as their male counterparts.

And now the legend continues.

# Chapter One

## We Gotta Get Outa This Place

Well I can say without hesitation that I was ready for a change. I had been a part of the system and an avid pursuer of the American dream for many, many years. I was always working for something, although at times I couldn't put my finger on what it was exactly.

After a fairly successful college career at University of Virginia, finally getting my degree in accounting, I did what most of my college buddies did. I joined a very large and frankly stuffy accounting firm in Chicago. Money was good, even for a rookie, and it was a prestigious job. I felt like I had earned it since I was one of the few guys out of school who had spent considerable time in the computer lab after regular classes. I had a solid understanding of all the new technology that was at that time called "data processing".

I know, I know, boring as watching golf on tv, right? Sorry Tiger!

Ultimately my hard work paid off and I even got lucky in my love life and met Lisa-Michelle, who would become my wife and fellow traveler. I knew darned well she outclassed me but somehow, I also knew she would be my life long "trophy wife". And I don't just mean that because she was and is beautiful. Nope I realized right away that she would help me chart a productive life but ensure that I always took time to actually enjoy it.

And I did enjoy the fruits of my labor with the firm for many years. In fact, I had a great condo and nice Mercedes only a couple of years old to attest to the fact that I had arrived. But as a corporate machine, I was running out of gas. I was about to make partner and I knew that would mean an even a greater commitment to the company, who had been good to me. So just as I was about to reach the pinnacle…I bailed.

I guess Lisa-Michelle, whom I call Lee, understood that I felt stagnant and agreed to relocate with me to Virginia Beach. I'd always been drawn to the ocean and had visited this tourist area several times for long weekends while going to UVA. There's just something about the sound and smell of the ocean that brought out a certain creativity in me. I suppose it's that way it is with many people.

Oh yes, I forgot to introduce myself. My name is Greg Priestly. At least for now. More on that later.

Of course, after the move, I had to earn a living and decided to start my own accounting firm to serve the Tidewater region of Virginia. There was tremendous growth in that area at the time and I felt certain that with my background, I could scare up enough clients to get by. But my safety net as I worked on my new business was the job Lee was able to find with an advertising agency in Norfolk. Lee had a talent for graphics and a real understanding of how to build a marketing campaign. She got her job offer during the initial interview. That's my girl! (oh sorry…. it's "woman" of course, although somehow that just sounds funny.)

So, we found a place to live as close to the beach as we could afford and began the process of building a life where I could be a combination of zipped up accountant and weekend beach bum. I was probably better at the latter but, as I said, my credentials at the former were a better intro for finding clients.

Years passed and, as my business built, I added several clients each year and of course employees. I had a dear friend once who pointed out that the best days of a business owner's career were in the first few months when there are no clients and no employees. Ironic. What is a business without clients or employees? He couldn't have been more right, but I soldiered on anyway.

To be sure I found the work pretty tedious and, while I was good to my employees, I never felt like I was a particularly good manager. The company flourished, but I didn't believe I had much of a head for business. It was almost as if I was successful in spite of myself.

I might have gone bonkers but for one frequent activity. Without fail Lee and I would head for the beach, at least on the weekends. During the summer we could enjoy swimming in the ocean of course but even during the winter we would walk at the water's edge and talk about hopes and dreams. It was almost like a dating ritual. We grew even closer as a couple during those walks.

In relatively short order I found myself spending more time watching the surfers who amazingly found waves to ride near a place called Rudee Inlet. You wouldn't imagine Virginia Beach as being a surfing mecca, but I found out pretty quickly that the surfers who had enough patience could find a ride on any given day on any given beach. I also found out that there was an annual surfing challenge on Virginia Beach called the East Coast Surfing Championship. Lee and I made a point to attend that event every year. Back to surfing in minute.

While I was building my accounting practice, Lee had been promoted a couple of times and now owned her own agency. We were both making good money, but I soon realized that together we had recreated the life we had before moving to the beach. I wasn't sure that's what I had in mind at all.

One Saturday afternoon in May, Lee was stuck at her office working on an upcoming pitch to a potentially large client in Richmond. I decided to head for the beach anyway and was naturally drawn to the surfing area. Most of the surfers were quite young, although there was an occasional geezer out there unwilling or unable to give up the sport he loved and thereby give in to advancing age. I had to admit I totally got it. Reminded me of a song by Don Henley called "I Will Not Go Quietly".

I decided to approach one of the older surfers to find out a bit more about what motivated him. I'm really not sure why. As I approached him on the beach, I tried to find a way to introduce myself in a way that didn't present me as some sort of surf groupie, but pretty much failed.

"Excuse, me, I couldn't help but notice you caught some fairly good waves out there. Must be kind of challenging," I blurted out sounding every bit as nerdy as I felt.

"Nah, if you pay attention to what the ocean is telling you, you can find a way grab one."

"I'm sorry, I'm Greg, Greg Priestly," I said sticking out my hand, "I guess I'm just a would-be surfer at heart," I admitted.

"I'm Joey Richfield. Folks call me JR," he responded completing the handshake.

"I didn't mean to interrupt your day, JR," I said. "If you're busy I understand."

"It's cool. I was about to take a break anyway. Are you a tourist or what?"

Sizing JR up I figured him to be in his 50s. He had one of those enviable tans everyone wanted before they figured out how bad tanning was for your skin. He was extremely fit, I assumed because of surfing, and had longish dark hair with streaks of gray. I had the strangest feeling we'd met before. No matter.

"Actually, I'm a local," I answered, "I live further on up the beach. I've just grown really interested in surfing lately."

"So, you should try it!"

"Seems like I might be a little old to start now," I said hoping I didn't insult the man, "Watching you I guess you've been surfing since you were a kid."

"Your guess would be way off. I actually only started about 5 years ago. I gave myself my first board on my 50th birthday in fact," JR responding smiling broadly.

I think JR got a kick out of my assumption that he had great surfing skills.

"Wow…good for you!" could I have sounded any more goofy?

"I was kind of like you, just watching from the beach. When I turned 50, I started to wonder if my proverbial ship had sailed and decided to prove to myself, I could still learn new things."

Listening to JR talk I quickly realized that this was a professional man. Someone with a white- collar job but who wanted more out of life. I certainly understood that pull.

"So, what do you do, Greg?" JR asked.

"Hate to even admit it but I'm an accountant. I have my own firm," I replied.

"Well I can top that as far as hating to admit it. I'm an attorney. Not the fun kind either, just corporate."

We both had a laugh at our own expense. Somehow, I couldn't imagine JR being called 'Joey' at the office. Might be a name he uses on the beach when some schmuck comes up and interrupts his surfing.

"Say JR, do you have time for beer?"

"I'll make time."

There was a beachfront tiki bar at a hotel near where we were standing so we headed up towards the boardwalk. JR planted the nose of his board in the soft sand in a position where he could see it from the bar. We found two stools with a pretty good view of the Atlantic and ordered a couple of drafts.

"So are you married," I asked for no particular reason.

"Used to be. Didn't work out. I now have a 'girlfriend'," he said almost seeming embarrassed by the term, "How about you?"

"Married, very happily by the way, for more years than I'll admit to. Her name is Lisa-Michelle. I call her Lee"

"It's good to run into someone who made marriage work. I guess I just didn't invest the time in the relationship."

"So, back to surfing, can I pick your brain a bit?" figuring it was a good time to change the subject.

"Of course, but I reserve the right to object," JR said trying to make a lawyer joke. I chuckled to be polite.

"What drew you to this sport in particular?"

"It seemed like everywhere I went there were stories of legendary surfers, big waves and good times. So, I started hanging around the beach like you're doing, and asking questions. Finally found a guy willing to give me some fundamental lessons, even though I was older. I took my share of ribbing from him and some of the young dudes on the beach, so I had to try a lot harder to get up on the board and get any kind of decent ride."

"You look like you are damned good at it now," I said.

"Well I had to force myself to surf almost every day, coming to the beach before sun-up so that I could get to the office on time. Over the course of several months I just figured out how to use my body and my board to get the best ride possible."

"I guess you don't take much ribbing now," I ventured.

"Wrong. They still call me the 'old man', but I really don't mind anymore. Most of the young guys are good dudes I found out. At first, I was jealous of their youth but finally decided I wouldn't want to be their age now. Too many challenges."

"Sounds like you were following your dream."

"You could say that. You must have something like that."

"I have this germ of an idea of having my own beach bar somewhere even warmer than here. Not a very realistic dream. I've already uprooted Lee once in our life together. I don't know how it would go over now."

"My advice to you is to keep your dream at the forefront and slowly let Lee into it. Most women want to know those things. But who am I to give relationship advice? My marriage didn't work."

"You make a good point anyway," I said.

We finished our beer and continued to chat until we agreed it was time to head home. I suggested we get together once in a while and talk about 'old man' things or surfing or how women think or whatever came to mind.

"As long as there is cold beer," JR said laughing. I had a business card in a belt pack I had with me and handed it to JR. He promised he would call in a week or so.

We shook hands and JR went to retrieve his board. I walked on down the boardwalk towards home. I was convinced that I had found a friend that I could use to bounce ideas off of. JR might even be willing to help me learn to surf, although I wasn't certain that was as important to me as it was to him. I kind of wished I could find a way to enjoy the 'legacy' of surfing as JR called it, be a part of the culture and not necessarily have to exert myself. *Jeez what a wimp you are,* I told myself.

I knew I had a lot of thinking to do.

# Chapter Two

## The Slow Build

Lee was back from the office when I got home and in the process of making us a stir fry. She had become something of a health nut in the past couple of years and knew exactly how to put together just the right ingredients to make a meal healthy but also taste like a gourmet offering. I knew I had found the right woman all those years ago.

Not to say that I wasn't a good cook in my own right. Trouble was I specialized in things like chili, spaghetti sauce and all things fattening. To her credit Lee would at least try my creations. Just not much of any of them. What I *had* perfected were my chicken wings. I could make those little critters crispy and really tasty, with a hint of barbeque and sometimes a shot of Old Bay. I was really proud of that creation. but Lee only ever had one or sometimes two if I poured her a second beer.

As usual, Lee had music blaring on the stereo. Her tastes ran to Police and the Cars…all that new wave stuff. For me it was Beachboys, maybe some Beatles. Since the onset of my obsession with surfing I had even come to like the Ventures, Surfaris and Jan and Dean. Then of course there was Dick Dale and the Deltones. Good grief, I'm really showing my age.

I can actually remember when I first heard "Wipeout". It was a new record then. Okay forget that I admitted that.

Lee was dancing around the stove to the sound of "Don't Stand So Close to Me" when I approached her from behind and gave her what I thought was a loving bear hug. I know you saw this coming, but Lee's reaction was anything but loving. In fact, she elbowed me in the stomach, later claiming she thought I was an intruder. Sure! Won't make that mistake again.

Quickly recovering from her apparent surprise, she asked, "So what have you been up to today?"

"Had an interesting day. I went down to watch the surfers the other side of the pier and ran into a guy who was closer to my age. Great surfer. At least it looked like that to me."

"Did you get a chance to talk?"

"Yep, in fact we had a beer together and he talked about his start at surfing. Interesting story. He didn't even pick up a board until he was 50."

"Wow, that's impressive."

"His name is Joey something or other and he goes by JR. He said he's a corporate lawyer."

"I would think a surfing corporate attorney in his 40s is a bit rare," Lee said, stating the obvious.

"Well after a failed marriage I think he was trying to recapture some of his youth. I guess surfing had been his personal fantasy pursuit."

"I suppose everyone has at least one at some point in their life," Lee offered, beginning to take up the stir fry. Normally we ate casually at the kitchen island. We vowed not to have the tv on during dinner so that we could catch up on each other's lives.

"How is your proposal coming along?" I decided to open the conversation.

"It's been a slow process because the campaign is multi-media, but I think we have a fair shot of winning the business."

I had long known that Lee's life fantasy had been to produce film or tv projects. She certainly had the eye and a keen sense of how to make a point visually. I knew absolutely nothing about video or movie production, of course, but I did know that if Lee set her mind to it, she would make it happen no matter what the goal.

After hearing more about the firm, they were pursuing in Richmond and the approach her agency was taking, I decided to revisit the discussion I had with JR on the beach.

"You know JR asked me what my personal life fantasy was. I was kind of hesitant to talk about it, particularly since you and I hadn't had a chance have that discussion, but he pressed me a bit."

"Well I'm eager to hear about it, as long as it doesn't involve disrupting our whole life. Been there, done that."

"It would never happen, so I don't think you have to worry about that," I said deciding that putting my cards on the table right then might be counterproductive.

"Come on Greg, you're holding back, I know you are," Lee said, playing with her stir fry.

As long as I live, I don't think I'll ever forget how that conversation evolved that evening.

"It's really just about getting out of accounting and opening my own bar/restaurant. Not much different than many people, I guess. At least guys."

"From what I hear that's a dangerous business. Cash driven and prone to failure because of profit walking out the door with the employees," Lee said, ever the analyst and pragmatist in our relationship.

"I know, I've heard that myself, but my vision goes a little beyond that. Recently I've been asking myself "what's next?".

"Um, what do you mean, Greg?" she asked, at first not looking up from the stir fry. Finally, she peered at me with a quizzical look on her face. "What's really on your mind, Greg?"

Not wanting to totally scare the bejesus out of her, I proceeded cautiously.

"Well, we've been here for twenty years and I sure would like to talk about a change of scenery," I said, venturing carefully.

"You mean you'd like to move to Newport News or maybe Norfolk?" Lee asked. "The real estate market is pretty good right now, so we can probably afford a bigger home in one of the nicer neighborhoods."

"Um…not exactly what I had in mind. I've been doing accounting for most of my life and I guess for many of those years I've had a completely different dream," I said still cautiously, watching the look on her face change.

"Come on, Greg, why haven't you mentioned this before?"

"Because I thought it would seem frivolous and unrealistic."

"You might as well tell me what you have in mind. I need to know so that I can formulate an appropriate counterpoint," Lee said, rather appropriately. "You want to move, open a bar…what's the bottom line?".

I was hesitant to go on at this point, but I was in too deep.

"Lee, have you ever fantasized about being a completely different person with a different past and totally different goals?"

Lee was getting confused at this point and appeared to be losing her appetite, whatever that looks like.

"What's wrong with Greg Priestly? After all that's the man I married, and he seems like a pretty good guy. And I thought he was happy."

"I am happy, Lee. At least mostly."

I couldn't tell if Lee as simply concerned or getting annoyed.

"Is it me, Greg?"

"Oh no Lisa-Michelle! I should have told you right up front that you are the one aspect of my life I'm truly happy with."

"You never call me Lisa-Michelle anymore unless there is bad news. Did you lose the business or rob a bank or something?"

As if those two possibilities were equally distasteful.

"Of course not. Anyway, if it was anything like that, you'd know…you always know."

"Then what?"

Okay here goes.

"Well since I was a teenager, I think I've had this alter ego. It started when my folks almost moved to Florida. My dad's dream was always to live there, enjoy the great weather and pursue his dream of opening a convenience store or neighborhood bar or something. I never understood why other than how tough it was working in a steel mill."

"Okay," Lee said." Let's get to your fantasy." She sat back from the kitchen island and nearly lost her balance on the stool. Not good.

"Well, my folks used to take us to Florida once a year on vacation and I began to notice the teenaged boys on the beach with their huge surfboards. They all seemed to be perfectly tanned and physically fit. Getting to know some of them during vacation of course, many were one can short of a six pack, but that's neither here nor there."

"Uh-huh."

"But over time I'd fall asleep dreaming about learning to surf, growing my hair and basically hanging out at the beach. Of course, making a living never crossed my mind, but the fantasy was vivid. I even made up a name for myself."

"Puddinhead?" Lee chuckled but was clearly mocking me.

"I tried out several combinations of names that sounded like a surfer and finally landed on Corky Sandoval."

"You're not Hispanic. Isn't Sandoval Hispanic?"

"You're right but that's beside the point. I was inventing a whole new me. I even made up stories about moving from the West Coast after having lived the life of a surf bum. I must have reworked and tweaked Corky's background forty or fifty times and eventually he seemed very real to me. I even introduced myself to the kids I met in Florida as Corky just to try out the "other me" persona. They all seemed to buy it so in that sense, I am Corky to some degree. See what I mean?"

"Nope," Lee said pushing back from the island a little further and crossing her arms.

We sat there for a moment and I saw a look of confusion on Lee's face. I could sense she was getting agitated, more so than I anticipated. I think she thought our entire life was in question. I really didn't want to hurt her but thought she should know about my little (well, okay, not so little) fantasy. I thought it was harmless. From her facial expression and body language I could see she didn't agree.

"Time out."

Lisa-Michelle always used those two words to indicate that the conversation was over, at least for the moment. It usually meant that she was either steamed with me and didn't want to say something she would later regret, or she was confused. I think this might have been a combination of both.

So, I clammed up and we went on with our evening.

The next morning, I woke up with the radio alarm playing *Wouldn't It Be Nice* of all things. Of course, it had to be the Beachboys. I love the Beachboys but this particular morning it just pointed out that I hadn't made much headway the prior evening.

I have to say I was really surprised when Lee brought up the discussion at breakfast.

"So, what's the bottom line on your Corky fantasy, Greg?," Lee asked over eggs-benedict. She made killer eggs-benedict, by the way.

"Are you sure you want to know?"

"Well, you took it this far and it seems to mean a lot to you, so shoot," she replied, looking a little more prepared for the rest of the fantasy than she had the prior evening.

I began laying out a vision of liquidating our worldly goods, moving to a more tropical location and beginning again. As I had told her before, for several years I had wanted to open my own bar and grill. As my vision for a beachfront tiki bar evolved, so did the fantasy of a new life as Corky. Eventually I imagined owning" Corky's," a bar with a surfing theme. I would assume the persona of Corky and base the surroundings on his legacy of winning surf competitions back in the day.

"So, you mean to say you would give up everything about our life now to *become* this surfer character full time? What about our families and friends? Would we be able to earn a living running a bar?" Lee asked. I knew she would have a million more questions.

I had to admit I hadn't thought the idea through completely and didn't have immediate answers.

"I think if we put our heads together, we could make a go of it," said in my best sales mode, "I mean, I'm an accountant and your business is about promoting things. Surely, we're smart enough to pull it off."

"Would it mean I have to give up my identity and play some sort of character?".

"Not necessarily, but it could be fun for you too. You could be an ex-hooker with a heart of gold," I said facetiously.

"No, no, no!"

"I was only kidding, Lee but you could spin a little background for yourself that filled in some of the blanks in Corky's story."

"What if someone outed you? Maybe someone from the old firm or one of your current clients?"

"Well, we would just have to cross that bridge when we come to it, or as Buffet said, "*burn that bridge when we come to it,*" I said, chuckling.

I could tell no amount of levity was getting through.

"Look, Lee, just do me a favor and sleep on it. I'm ready for a new adventure but if you decide you aren't, we'll just forget it."

Lisa-Michelle had a blank look on her face but finally said, "I guess I owe you that much. Let's talk again tomorrow. I can't get my head around it right now, but I'll think it through."

I kissed her on the cheek, not venturing a real kiss and she flinched just a bit. Not a good sign.

"Thanks, honey," I said, settling for a small win.

# Chapter Three

## I'll Have the Mahi

As I said, the next day was a 'school day', as we used to kid, so both Lee and I needed to head off to work as normal. Before we kissed goodbye and wished each other a good day, Lee suggested we meet at an ocean front bar called Mahi Mahs for a cocktail after work. I readily accepted, in part because I knew she wouldn't be too hard on me in public.

When I walked in at five-thirty, Lee was already there and had ordered our usual drinks. With me, it was a Bombay Sapphire and tonic and she preferred a dirty vodka martini, Tito's if you please. That was a good sign as was the normal warm smile she had on her face when we reunited after work. I was growing hopeful.

"Well, Lee, have you done some more thinking about our discussion?"

Taking a sip of her martini Lee looked at me and paused just a bit too long in my mind. I braced for a wholesale rejection.

"Here's the way I feel," Lee began, "We've had a hell of a ride so far and there are only so many years left."

"Jeez, Lee, I hope there are twenty or more," I said.

"Beside the point for this discussion. I'm not being morbid, just realistic. Anyway, hear me out, will you?"

"Sorry."

"I think it is more than a little weird. I also think it could mean we lose everything we've worked so hard for."

My heart sank.

"With that said I agree that a new adventure is appealing to me too, but with certain stipulations."

"I'm listening." Using my Frasier Crane voice.

"First, if I'm going to be part of building these new personas and the business, I want a say in every major decision."

"Of course." No hesitation on my part. I always thought she had a sharper business mind than mine anyway.

"Second, we have to run the place like a real business. I mean things like no free drinks for the boys."

"What boys?"

Lee looked at me with a little disdain. "You're missing my point. You know as well as I do that there *will* be boys. Hangers on, frequent flyers. I'm sure you know what I mean, right?"

"Right. Anything else?"

"Yes, I want you to promise if you're busted, you're busted. If someone figures out you are really Greg Priestly or that Corky what's his name is just a character, you won't lie about it. I mean you can explain it away as a marketing gimmick or something, but I just don't want to be part of a huge lie and have to remember all the details all the time. Too much stress and leaving stress behind is part of the goal isn't it?"

"It is. Might be the most important part in fact." I replied sensing real progress.

"Oh, and one more thing," Lee continued, "In private I refuse to call you Corky. You'll always be Greg at home. So, do we have a deal?".

She held out her hand and I gladly shook it, as if she were a client rather than my wife.

"Deal!" I replied, all the while noticing that she wasn't beaming with anticipation. More like half-smiling in resignation.

And so, began the task of taking apart one life and beginning another one. I had no idea what a big job it would be. I would soon find out.

# Chapter Four

## The JR Effect

The next day JR called as if on cue and we decided to head over to the same beachfront bar about 5:30. Frankly, I was happy to hear from my new friend. I was eager to tell him about my discussions with Lee.

JR walked in and I immediately noticed he looked a little worse for the wear. Most notably he had some sort of abrasion on the left side of his face and what appeared to be a large bruise on his left forearm.

"What the hell happened to you?" I asked, expecting to hear about some senior citizen bar fight.

"Man, I'm almost embarrassed to tell you, but I had a really bad wipeout yesterday and took a header into the sand. I felt like I had no control at all."

"You're kidding, in this surf?"

"Yep and the weird thing is it wasn't even a particularly big break. Nothing about that freakin' wave would make you think you might lose it," he admitted.

"So, why do you think it happened?" I continued.

"Only thing I can figure out is that my mind was wandering. No matter what they tell you about surfing becoming one of your muscle memories, you still have to think about each ride. At least I do," he admitted.

"You deserve a beer, and I'm buying," I offered.

We settled in over a couple of Coronas and I found myself filling JR in on my talks with Lee.

"Boy, you are one brave dude. Do you think she'll actually go through with it?" JR asked.

"I really don't know but I guess I didn't expect her to do what she did. Now I'm getting kind of scared," I replied.

"I can only imagine. If I thought about leaving my law practice to take a whole different route, I'd be having second thoughts too."

"But I'm also afraid of not grabbing the opportunity. Last time I looked I wasn't getting any younger".

"Let me ask you something," JR said, "Do you have in mind how this Corky character would have evolved into...well...you?".

"No, not really. In my mind he is just an 18 or 19-year-old surfer kid with a good heart and high expectations', I chuckled at the mental image.

"Well if the back story on Corky is believable you have to play it out...at least in your mind."

"Point taken," I said pondering the wisdom of JRs comment.

"I guess if I were you, I'd at least put an outline of his life with the high points and low points down on paper so it's clear in your mind at least if not your wife's. If you want to become the surfer dude, you have to know everything about him."

I bought JR another beer in appreciation of his sage advice and then headed back home to do a little creative thinking.

After all Corky couldn't be 18 forever, even if I had wanted to be at that age.

When I got home, Lee was working at the little office area we had set up for her. Regardless of what we did with the Corky dream, Lee was determined to win the big contract. I totally understood that goal. It would also help us financially since she would give herself a large bonus if the deal was closed.

"Hey Lee, I want to work some this evening too. Are you okay if we just order something to eat, maybe even pizza?" I asked, knowing fully that she might protest the fatty, unhealthy option.

"Fine by me," she said, surprisingly," I have too much to do to fight that suggestion."

"I get that, "I said, "I'll take care of it and then get to work myself."

Clearly distracted, Lee asked if it was for some new client at the accounting firm.

"Not exactly," I replied ambiguously. She didn't notice or didn't care.

I called the pizza shop on the corner and set aside the money to pay the delivery person including a liberal tip and then sat down at my desk to consider an outline of the Corky story. After a while I realized that an outline wouldn't adequately portray a persona I'd had in my mind since I was a teenager. So, I began to put words to paper imagining the person I wanted to be as he moved through his early life. It was a hell of an exercise.

# Chapter Five

## Daytona Days and Nights

Corky woke up on a Saturday morning feeling a bit disoriented. He knew he hadn't had too much to drink the night before. In fact, it was just the right amount. He'd had an odd dream and it haunted him a bit. But let's let him tell the story.

I couldn't shake the image of an older man sitting at a desk and writing something that included my name. I don't have any idea what he was writing about me or why, but the dream seemed very real. Oh well, there's no explaining that sort of thing is there?

Our team had had a really good Christmas. Gabe, my Hawaiian best friend whose real name was Kaapo, had surprised us with some very impressive pictures of Duke, Alexa, Stacy and me riding a really nice wave. All of us were blown away by his eye for action. I was proud of my buddy. Alexa and Stacy were two of the finest surfers I had ever met. Never mind that they were females. Duke was pretty much my equal at surfing if not my better. We had competed in some east coast events and usually I got the best of him. But at any moment it could go either way and we both knew it.

And then there was Abby. This red headed former cheerleader had joined Gabe and I for a cross country excursion back in California. Abby was a writer who was keeping a journal on our travels and minding our mascot Skipper, a Jack Russel, Boston Terrier mix. His contribution to our team was to keep our spirits up then eat, poop and sleep. Nice job and he did it well.

As winter slowly turned to spring, we all realized we had to make some decisions, some of which were going to be tough. I think all of us had the desire to keep moving to see new places and surf new breaks, but life in Daytona had become pretty appealing. We were all working, and the surf shop was doing great. Andy, the shop owner, was a as happy as I'd ever seen him and my surfboard line, CorkBoards ™), had really taken off. I say "my surfboard line" knowing full well that I had little to do with the design and manufacturing. I did have to take some credit for coaching the dude who made the boards. He was a surfer, but Andy had asked him to try to tailor the boards so that I approved. Felt like a big shot until I realized the guy knew a lot more about what works than I did. But it was more or less my name on the boards, so I at least took each new design out for a test ride.

I thought it might make sense to call a "family meeting" to discuss next steps. We all had different shifts at our jobs, so it took some doing to find a time when all of us were available. Finally, 11pm on a Thursday evening was selected. Not ideal but we were all night creatures to one extent or the other. That is all except Abby, of course, who rivaled Ben Franklin in her early to bed, early to rise routine. You have to remember that as a confirmed vegetarian and health nut she was sometimes a little over the top with her habits. Good thing she was cute.

On that Thursday we all sat down in the living room of our little home and began to bring each other up to date on recent developments. Seems as though Duke actually had a knack for sales, and he had surpassed all other sales reps at the furniture store during the holiday season. Quite frankly I never saw that coming. He'd made such a big deal out of how he hated the idea of working in his dad's store. But I was happy for him.

Everyone else offered up a story or two about how they had spent their time in Daytona Beach and to a person agreed that they felt really at home in this Florida town. That was part of the problem. We had promised before Christmas that we would continue our travels after the holidays. I had a feeling everyone was getting a little too comfortable.

I suppose I was eager to move on. That said, I really hated the idea of disappointing Andy. The shop had hit new levels of success. When I joined the sales team at Jack's Surf and Sail Andy had promoted me as a big deal surfer from California who had won some significant competitions. The uptick in business in my opinion wasn't because of my phony baloney reputation but the way Andy had leveraged it. He was a real businessman with a keen understanding of what sold and what didn't. I had the hint of an idea about what might soften the blow of him hearing we were moving on but didn't share it with the others immediately.

We decided to take a vote on whether we would head out on the road as planned and if so when. I was surprised to find that everyone voted to move on. The only point of contention was the "when" question. Abby, Alexa and Stacy wanted to leave in a couple of weeks and head north to New England. Duke felt like he owed his dad a little more notice. I was inclined to agree with Duke that our departure shouldn't come before about a month so that our employers had time to adjust and even hire replacements. As for Gabe he fell asleep and Skipper, while wide awake, offered no opinion. He did have to pee though.

So, we compromised and agreed to three weeks and then a departure north. Our lease was month to month so the landlord shouldn't be too surprised. At Elinor Village where we lived, they even rented by the week to tourists. No issue there.

Next morning, I pulled Duke and Gabe aside to run an idea by them. I tried to do it discreetly so that the ladies didn't think it was some male conspiracy. It wasn't. My idea was to present Andy with a proposition that we publicized our trip north to find good surf break and let it be a promotional gimmick for the shop. "Corkboard Team Tour" or "Jacks Surf Team" or something like that might drive business to Daytona and finally to Jack's. It was an idea where all of us benefited. Who knew if Andy would agree…but worth a try.

If it was going to work, each of us would have to make a contribution, even beyond surfing well enough to win some competitions. Duke, Gabe and I decided to mull over the idea and then call another family meeting to bring everyone into the picture and inventory our non-surfing skills. After all, we needed to make a business case to Andy (aren't you impressed by my newfound business savvy? I know I am).

After a couple of days, I asked everyone to meet again. This time it was Saturday night and Abby had to work later so we put the meeting off until Sunday morning. No one really wanted to get up early, so we decided to meet over breakfast at 10am. Stacy offered to make some eggs and bacon. Bless her heart (see how I picked up the southern lingo!).

That morning we explained the idea to the ladies and asked that each of us suggest what contributions we might make toward the effort. I made a point that we had to look like a legitimate surf team, so our efforts needed to be well coordinated. Of course, Gabe offered to be the tour manager and arrange for us to enter competitions along the way.

Everyone offered up ideas of how they could contribute. Maybe the most surprising thing about that meeting was finding out that Alexa considered herself a pretty competent artist and wanted to get into promotional work after enjoying herself for a while. She made a point that, if Andy wanted us to do it, we would need promotional material including a team logo. I reminded her that if we chose a CorkBoards ™ team name there was the surfer logo. But she convinced us that we had to expand on that to promote the actual tour. Now where did that all come from? Hot girl, great surfer and business head as well? I was amazed and maybe a little infatuated.

Since everyone seemed in favor of the idea, I took on the task of telling Andy, or proposing the tour to him. I didn't usually work on Sunday but went in that afternoon. Andy was surprised to see me since he knew I usually tried to spend as much time catching waves as I could on Sundays. Andy had another guy on the floor so when I asked him if we could talk, he was able to show me back to the office. I must admit he had a worried look on his face, maybe anticipating I was resigning.

I felt compelled to say, "Andy, I don't have any bad news to deliver…at least I don't think it's bad news."

"Well that's a relief," Andy sighed.

"I have an idea I want to tell you about. I think it would be good for both the shop and for me, but it would take me off the sales floor, at least for a while."

"Darn, Corky, you know you're our best sales rep. Clients are used to coming in to see you and lot of them bring money," he chuckled but nervously.

"I know Andy, but you've always known I've been on a quest to find the best breaks. Right now, I'm working on the east coast but eventually I should head back to California," I reminded him.

"I guess you made that clear, but I was hoping it wouldn't be for a good while. After all, it's peak season."

"And that's one reason behind this idea," I said watching his face closely.

I began to lay out the concept of a team tour promoting and apparently sponsored by Jack's and CorkBoards ™. I explained to him that our crew would do most of the work but that I needed his blessing to enter challenges as we traveled. I even suggested I might have a good chance at winning the East Coast Surfing Championship up in Virginia Beach. After all, I had surfed there and knew exactly what to expect. I told him that Alexa mentioned a place in New England that had an almost west coast break.

After a while you could tell that the wheels started turning in Andy's mind, trying to determine how we could make the tour payoff for the shop and the board design company.

"Corky I do have to ask what all of this would cost," the look of worry returning the Andy's face, "I don't think the shop could take the dip in sales *and* a big sponsorship fee."

"We've all been saving for the time we moved on and restarted our little journey. That's the cool part. If you invest anything it would be a small amount. We're willing to pay our own way and still promote the shop."

You could tell that Andy was starting to get the picture. After all, a lot of folks from further north vacationed on the east coast of Florida, so promoting the best surf shop on the Atlantic side was bound to drive in some business. Also, the locals would have something to talk about. We had already decided that we would call Andy no less than every other day so that he could post updates on a.... well....real corkboard. So, following the team might encourage people to come to the shop more frequently. Andy could also spin some tales along the way.

"What are you thinking of calling the team…assuming we can work this out?" Andy asked.

"I thought we'd get the best bang for our buck, so to speak, by calling it "The CorkBoards™ Surf Team Tour sponsored by Jack's Surf and Sail, Daytona Beach, Florida". It's a long name but Alexa says she can make us some sort of promo sign and some other stuff that will work with that. I just want the shop to benefit. I feel pretty bad about leaving. But think of it like this, if we do well, when we return we may draw more people in the late season than even this past year," I said, hoping Andy thought the loss of sales reps was balanced out by the benefit of the promotion.

"When would you head out?" Andy asked as expected.

"We'd be here for another 3 weeks for sure," I assured him.

"Corky, if you don't mind, I'd like to sleep on it."

"Of course, boss."

"You know I don't like being called boss," Andy reminded me. He was smiling, though, which made me feel a bit better.

"Of course, Andy," I corrected myself.

The shop was getting busy by this point and Andy felt like he should get back out to the sales floor. I offered to stick around and help for a while, but he said, "Maybe you should head out and do some practicing. The surf looks pretty promising today."

Good sign.

When I got back to the house only Gabe was there.

"How did Andy take it?" he asked.

"Well I think he understands how it might be good for all of us, if we do it right. But it's going to take all of us doing our part. A lot of it is going be on you, you being the business manager and all," I reminded Gabe.

"I can handle it…. the 'gift of Gabe' will take us a long way," Gabe said always referring back to his own pat-on-the-back motto.

The next day was Monday and I had a shift starting at 1pm. When I got to the shop Andy wasn't there. For some reason that bothered me. Another sales guy named Barry had opened the shop and was waiting on a couple of cute girls when I walked in. After he managed to sell them a couple of t-shirts each and getting one girl's number, I asked him if he knew where Andy was.

"Not a clue, dude. He just asked me to open the shop and then turn it over to you when you got here. I don't think he's sick or anything. Seemed like he had something to do, maybe for Daisy," Barry responded.

Oh yes, in case I haven't mentioned it, Daisy was Andy's lady.

Andy showed up about 2:00. The shop was quiet at the time, so he called me over to the register and said, "Okay, I'm down with it, man. If we can work out the details and I can have approval of the promotional material I would even like to invest a little."

"Andy, you will have complete say on the brands, how we talk about the shop and so forth. I should have told you that yesterday. You're the man."

Andy stuck out his hand and we perfectly executed the brother shake. I was so relieved I felt like kissing him, but luckily had better sense.

I couldn't wait to get the team together and share the news.

# *Billboard*  Year-End Hot 100 singles of 1968

| No | Title | Artist(s) |
|---|---|---|
| 1 | "Hey Jude" | *The Beatles* |
| 2 | "Love is Blue" | *Paul Mauriat* |
| 3 | "Honey" | *Bobby Goldsboro* |
| 4 | "(Sittin' On) The Dock of the Bay" | *Otis Redding* |
| 5 | "People Got to Be Free" | *The Rascals* |
| 6 | "Sunshine of Your Love" | *Cream* |
| 7 | "This Guy's in Love With You" | *Herb Alpert* |
| 8 | "The Good, the Bad and the Ugly" | *Hugo Montenegro* |
| 9 | "Mrs. Robinson" | *Simon & Garfunkel* |
| 10 | "Tighten Up" | *Archie Bell & the Drells* |
| 11 | "Harper Valley PTA" | *Jeannie C. Riley* |
| 12 | "Little Green Apples" | *O. C. Smith* |
| 13 | "Mony Mony" | *Tommy James and the Shondells* |
| 14 | "Hello, I Love You" | *The Doors* |
| 15 | "Young Girl" | *Gary Puckett & The Union Gap* |
| 16 | "Cry Like a Baby" | *The Box Tops* |
| 17 | "Stoned Soul Picnic" | *The 5th Dimension* |
| 18 | "Grazing in the Grass" | *Hugh Masekela* |
| 19 | "Midnight Confessions" | *The Grass Roots* |
| 20 | "Dance to the Music" | *Sly & the Family Stone* |
| 21 | "The Horse" | *Cliff Nobles* |
| 22 | "I Wish It Would Rain" | *The Temptations* |
| 23 | "La-La (Means I Love You)" | *The Delfonics* |
| 24 | "Turn Around, Look at Me" | *The Vogues* |
| 25 | "Judy in Disguise (With Glasses)" | *John Fred & His Playboy Band* |
| 26 | "Spooky" | *Classics IV* |
| 27 | "Love Child" | *The Supremes* |
| 28 | "Angel of the Morning" | *Merrilee Rush* |
| 29 | "The Ballad of Bonnie and Clyde" | *Georgie Fame* |
| 30 | "Those Were the Days" | *Mary Hopkin* |
| 31 | "Born to Be Wild" | *Steppenwolf* |
| 32 | "Cowboys to Girls" | *The Intruders* |
| 33 | "Simon Says" | *1910 Fruitgum Company* |
| 34 | "Lady Willpower" | *Gary Puckett & The Union Gap* |
| 35 | "A Beautiful Morning" | *The Rascals* |
| 36 | "The Look of Love" | *Sérgio Mendes* |
| 37 | "Hold Me Tight" | *Johnny Nash* |
| 38 | "Yummy Yummy Yummy" | *Ohio Express* |
| 39 | "Fire" | *The Crazy World of Arthur Brown* |
| 40 | "Love Is All Around" | *The Troggs* |
| 41 | "Playboy" | *Gene & Debbe* |
| 42 | "(Theme from) Valley of the Dolls" | *Dionne Warwick* |
| 43 | "Classical Gas" | *Mason Williams* |
| 44 | "Slip Away" | *Clarence Carter* |
| 45 | "Girl Watcher" | *The O'Kaysions* |
| 46 | "(Sweet Sweet Baby) Since You've Been Gone | *Aretha Franklin* |
| 47 | "Green Tambourine" | *The Lemon Pipers* |
| 48 | "1, 2, 3, Red Light" | *1910 Fruitgum Company* |
| 49 | "Reach out of the Darkness" | *Friend & Lover* |
| 50 | "Jumpin' Jack Flash" | *The Rolling Stones* |

1. "*Billboard Top 100 – 1968*"
(*https://web.archive.org/web/20101125102556/http://longboredsurfer.com/charts/196 8.php*). *Archived from the original  (http://longboredsurfer.com/charts/1968.php) on 2010-11-25. Retrieved  2011-01-05. Retrieved from "https://en.wikipedia. org/w/index.php?title=Billboard_Year- End_Hot_100_singles_of_1968&oldid=898781379".*

This list is of *Billboard* magazine's Top **Hot 100** songs of 1968.[1]

| 51 | "MacArthur Park" | *Richard Harris* |
|----|------------------|------------------|
| 52 | "Light My Fire" | *José Feliciano* |
| 53 | "I Love You" | *People!* |
| 54 | "Take Time to Know Her" | *Percy Sledge* |
| 55 | "Pictures of Matchstick Men" | *Status Quo* |
| 56 | "Summertime Blues" | *Blue Cheer* |
| 57 | "Ain't Nothing Like the Real Thing" | *Marvin Gaye & Tammi Terrell* |
| 58 | "I Got the Feelin'" | *James Brown* |
| 59 | "I've Gotta Get a Message to You" | *The Bee Gees* |
| 60 | "Lady Madonna" | *The Beatles* |
| 61 | "Hurdy Gurdy Man" | *Donovan* |
| 62 | "Magic Carpet Ride" | *Steppenwolf* |
| 63 | "Bottle of Wine" | *The Fireballs* |
| 64 | "Stay in My Corner" | *The Dells* |
| 65 | "Soul Serenade" | *Willie Mitchell* |
| 66 | "Delilah" | *Tom Jones* |
| 67 | "Nobody but Me" | *The Human Beinz* |
| 68 | "I Thank You" | *Sam & Dave* |
| 69 | "The Fool on the Hill" | *Sérgio Mendes* |
| 70 | "Sky Pilot" | *The Animals* |
| 71 | "Indian Lake" | *The Cowsills* |
| 72 | "I Wonder What She's Doing Tonight" | *Tommy Boyce & Bobby Hart* |
| 73 | "Over You" | *Gary Puckett & The Union Gap* |
| 74 | "Goin' Out of My Head/Can't Take My Eyes Off You" | *The Lettermen* |
| 75 | "Shoo-Be-Doo-Be-Doo-Da-Day" | *Stevie Wonder* |
| 76 | "The Unicorn" | *The Irish Rovers* |
| 77 | "You Keep Me Hangin' On" | *Vanilla Fudge* |
| 78 | "Revolution" | *The Beatles* |
| 79 | "Woman, Woman" | *Gary Puckett & The Union Gap* |
| 80 | "Elenore" | *The Turtles* |
| 81 | "White Room" | *Cream* |
| 82 | "You're All I Need to Get By" | *Marvin Gaye & Tammi Terrell* |
| 83 | "Baby, Now That I've Found You" | *The Foundations* |
| 84 | "Sweet Inspiration" | *The Sweet Inspirations* |
| 85 | "If You Can Want" | *Smokey Robinson and the Miracles* |
| 86 | "Cab Driver" | *The Mills Brothers* |
| 87 | "Time Has Come Today" | *The Chambers Brothers* |
| 88 | "Do You Know the Way to San Jose" | *Dionne Warwick* |
| 89 | "Scarborough Fair" | *Simon & Garfunkel* |
| 90 | "Say It Loud – I'm Black and I'm Proud" | *James Brown* |
| 91 | "The Mighty Quinn" | *Manfred Mann* |
| 92 | "Here Comes the Judge" | *Shorty Long* |
| 93 | "I Say a Little Prayer" | *Aretha Franklin* |
| 94 | "Think" | *Aretha Franklin* |
| 95 | "Sealed with a Kiss" | *Gary Lewis and the Playboys* |
| 96 | "Piece of My Heart" | *Big Brother and the Holding Company* |
| 97 | "Suzie Q." | *Creedence Clearwater Revival* |
| 98 | "Bend Me, Shape Me" | *The American Breed* |
| 99 | "Hey, Western Union Man" | *Jerry Butler* |
| 100 | "Never Give You Up" | *Jerry Butler* |

# Chapter Six

## The Real Work Begins

I was able to leave notes for everyone Monday evening to let them know things were looking good, but it was Tuesday afternoon before we could get the entire group together.

"So, Andy was okay with our plan?" said Alexa to start things off," I guess I'm just a bit surprised. I think he thinks of you as his actual brother, Corky."

"That may have actually helped," Duke pointed out.

"Look guys, we really have to use these three weeks to plan things out. All of us have to work our regular jobs so I think we may miss some sleep. I asked Gabe to plan the tour based on competitions along the way," I said.

"I'll have something in a couple of days," Gabe assured us.

"I'm going to start working on the tour logo and so forth," Alexa said, "Was Andy okay with the name?".

"Well I think I saw a little smile when I got to the part about sponsored by," I replied, "particularly when I said he really didn't have to invest anything if he didn't want to. He does want final approval on anything you come up with though."

"So, do you think he'll invest anyway?" Abby asked.

"He told me he would, but I wouldn't expect too much," I replied.

We met for a while longer before splitting up to work on our individual assignments or head out for the evening shift in Abby's case. I spent some time with Gabe looking over his notes about competitions. It was a handful gathering the information we needed and making a bunch of phone calls to surf shops and even city government in the places we thought there might be some action. In most cases, every little podunk town along the coastal route had some sort of competition. Most didn't offer any compensation, but some were at least notable enough that Jack's and CorkBoards ™ might benefit.

Gabe asked me a question that I am embarrassed to say hadn't occurred to me.

"Do you think we should be able take orders for CorkBoards ™ or even stuff from Jack's in each place you surf?" he asked.

"Wow, Gabe, great idea, but I have no idea how we might do that. I mean we can write up an order just like we do in the shop but we'll either have to mail or phone it in. It could take weeks for someone to get their order."

"True, but if we are honest right up front and they are impressed by the team they might not mind," Gabe replied quite logically.

I decided to run the idea by Andy the next day. I had to believe he had taken orders at some point during local meets and those in Florida. Maybe, maybe not, but might as well roll out the idea. When I got to the shop for my regular shift on Wednesday, I found one of the other sales guys running the floor and noticed Andy was sitting in his office. He appeared to be thoroughly engrossed in conversation with a dude in a suit. I found myself thinking *"boy sure hope that's not a cop"*.

I took a chance and walked on up to the door to Andy's office and poked my head in.

"Everything okay, boss?" I asked, knowing even as I said it I should have called him Andy.

"All okay, Corky, this is Roger Creighton. He runs a promotion firm. We're actually talking about your idea of a surf tour."

Roger offered up his hand and we exchanged acknowledgements. He seemed nice enough, business suit or not. Andy invited me to join the meeting and the conversation continued.

"Corky, Roger thinks you're on to something with the tour. The thing is, you'll be on the road and we're trying to drive business to the shop," Andy stated the obvious.

"Funny you mention that. Gabe came up with idea that we take orders on the road. Only issue is, how do we get them to the shop and how long will it take to ship stuff," I brought Andy up to date.

"Hmmmm.... interesting. Hadn't even thought of that," Andy said.

"I guess the only real way to do it is to call it in, write it up here in the shop and then the process is the same," Roger offered up.

"How about deposits? If we sell a Corkboard™, we really need a deposit," Andy pointed out.

"Well I suggest you appoint one of the team as treasurer. They can take the deposit, let the shop know it's in hand and send it in at the first opportunity," Roger continued his thought process.

"I think that would work nicely," Andy said getting more enthusiastic now that little details were being worked out.

"I think Stacy would make a great treasurer," I said, 'If that's okay with you, boss 'er Andy, I'll run it by her tonight."

"Proceed my good man," Andy replied with almost a theatrical flourish.

Over the next couple of weeks Roger turned out to be just the partner we needed. He had lots of practical experience promoting events and managed to keep us focused on our jobs while mapping out our overall strategy. To this day I don't know how Andy compensated him but at least that's something I didn't have to worry about.

One thing Roger did that I didn't anticipate, is insist that Duke and I be promoted as surf stars of sorts. He came up with an "East Coast meets West Coast" theme but played a bit fast and loose with what he called "the back story". If you took his promotion at face value, you'd think Duke and I had won lots of championships and you, the public, should be happy to see us perform. That promotion made Duke really squirm and I thought for a couple of days he might bow out. Only thing that saved the day was that Roger's promotions didn't really *say* anything specific about our backgrounds but only *implied* that we were top of the heap surfers.

Everyone did a bang-up job and finally we were ready to head out. Roger had worked with Gabe to map out the route and the events we would enter. He even managed to set up some radio interviews along the way. I only hoped I'd never be asked a direct question about the championships I had won. I was and am terrible at spinning tales. Honest. No, really!

We agreed to meet at the shop the morning we were planning to leave. I was blown away to find a Winnebago van waiting for us with *"The CorkBoards ™ Surf Team Tour sponsored by Jack's Surf and Sail, Daytona Beach Florida"* painted on the side. So, this is one way Andy helped sponsor the tour. The van was huge and would sleep the whole crew and even offered privacy for the girls. I found out later that the mobile home hadn't been out long. The first one rolled out in '66 so this was a pretty new van. I was really impressed. Must have cost a bundle. Roger pulled me aside and told me it was Andy's personal travel van. He was quickly becoming my hero. Must have been tough to let us head out with that beast. I assured him we would take care of his baby.

I guess I need to say that when Gabe and I set out on our little tour of America, I had no idea we would have the opportunity to do the things we've done since rolling into Daytona. I even thought we might be back in Cali by now, but here we were heading out of a promotional tour minus the Buggy. Even as we climbed onto the Winnebago, I wasn't at all sure I was ready for all the commercialism we were representing. Some days it even seemed a little sleazy. On the other hand, we were making a living of sorts, seeing more of the country and getting to hang out with our friends. I figured I could do it for a while anyway.

Before leaving we had to establish some routine mode of communication. Roger suggested that we call "home base," in other words the Jack's shop, every Tuesday, Thursday and Saturday morning at 11am unless we were competing. Seemed like a good plan so we all agreed to keep up that routine.

Duke was the only member of the tour team who had any experience driving a vehicle of the size of the Winnebago. He had driven trucks while delivering furniture for his dad. So, he was designated the captain of the SS Corkboard. Later I would get over my initial fears and drive part of the time but not before practicing in a big parking lot. I was surprised at how easily the big monstrosity was driven.

Seemed like we always had to have a name for everything, so we called our rolling home the only name that was obvious…. Winnie. *"Roll Winne roll!"* became our battle cry. The morning we left Duke even designated a team song. As we pulled away from the shop and waved goodbye to Andy and Roger, Duke blasted out "Surfin Safari" on the amazing sound system.

We were off to a good start. We could only hope our whole trip was as positive as that first day. Not so much.

# Chapter Seven

## The Pact, The Fort and the Journal

Early in our travels together our little surfin surfari had made a pact that anyone could suggest a diversion during the trip. There was a lot to see all over the country and we wanted to be able to enjoy as much of the landscape as possible. Abby and Gabe had been doing some reading on Florida history and had run across mention of an old fort called Castillo de San Marcos just up the highway in St. Augustine. (odd sentence) Abby was excited to tell us that the fort is the oldest and largest masonry fort on the mainland. Skipper just yawned at the revelation.

It was a painless side trip, so we decided to stop by the quaint oceanfront town and tour the fort as a group. I admit I wasn't thrilled with the prospect of touring a smelly old fort. That said I thought of myself as a team player and wanted to show some support for our "journalists" in the group. So off we went.

We ended up joining an actual guided tour of the fort. Most of the people touring with us were either older, maybe enjoying retirement, or young parents trying to expose their kids to some history. Duke and I must have been quite a sight in our baggie surf-shorts and t-shirts with the CorkBoards™ logo. Even so, everyone got along really well, and I managed to learn some things. I was kind of amazed to find out that the fort was built of coquina. While in Daytona I had learned that coquina was a kind of limestone that was made almost exclusively of broken shells.

Since Castillo was a fort, I wondered why the builders would have decided to use a porous material like coquina given the cannon fire it was built to withstand. The tour guide had a ready answer and congratulated me on a "great question". If the fort had been built with, let's say, granite he pointed out, a cannon ball could shatter the stone. Cannon balls fired into coquina tended to burrow into the material and just stay there. The guide was even able to show us where some cannon balls had struck the fort. Now I was getting interested.

Throughout the tour I noticed that Gabe was snapping pictures and Abby was taking a lot of notes. My friends and traveling companions obviously took their hobbies, or second callings or whatever seriously. I was impressed.

As things progressed, we were able to go inside the structure and look at the damp and barren rooms. I would hate to have been one of the soldiers who had to sleep in one of the "chambers" as the guide called them. I chuckled to myself thinking *on the other hand Gabe could sleep anywhere, even here.*

Soon the tour concluded, and we headed back to Winnie. All of us were talking about how amazing the fort had been. One thing struck us all as we walked the halls and barricades. There was clearly a feeling of spirituality in the old structure.

It was hard to describe but it was as if the ghosts of battles long past were there. Not at all scary, just inspiring, I guess.

As soon as we were back on the Winnebago Abby headed to her little "writing corner" and began putting pen to paper to describe our visit to St. Augustine. I made a mental note that we needed to spring for a typewriter for our budding author. I had read some of her journal along the way and just knew that Abby had a real way with words. I was looking forward to reading her account of our side-trip. I had no idea what her story about visiting Castillo de San Marcos would mean to our team and the tour. In fact, it would end up helping Andy and the shop.

Gabe on the other hand was lamenting to Stacy that he wasn't able to develop the pictures he shot right away. Our next stop being Jacksonville, maybe we could help him solve that problem. It was a modern and growing city and hopefully there were lots of camera shops. Gabe's photos would also play a huge part in making our tour a success.

Our focus right now, however, was to get going.

# Chapter Eight

## Roll, Winnie, Roll!

*"Jacksonville, I miss your morning light, I miss your steamy nights, oh my Jacksonville."*

From the song "Jacksonville" by Phil Perkins, as performed by The Child Band

I have to say I was really impressed by Duke's ability at driving Winnie. As time went on the team's confidence in his driving skills built up so that we could actually catch a nap sometimes. The first leg of our trip was pretty short, of course. It was only 40 or 50 miles from St. Augustine to Jacksonville. Gabe had planned out our participation in a small event at the adjacent Jacksonville Beach. Like a song on the radio called "Incense Peppermints" said, the event represented "little to win and nothing to lose".

We rolled into town just in time to register and shake a few hands. I guess we must have been quite a sight when we pulled up in our hulking Winnebago at a designated parking area. All around us were modest station wagons and small vans with boards strapped to the top. As I got out of Winnie, I immediately noticed that Duke had *"Surfin Surfari"* blasting on some outdoor speakers I didn't even know existed. I have to say I was a bit embarrassed.

Gabe quickly left the group and went to look for the registration desk. Meanwhile everyone else piled out of Winnie, we surveyed the break together and were reasonably impressed with the sets of waves we could see from the parking lot. Several surfers were out, and most were getting fair rides. I was eager to get wet but knew we had work to do before I could enjoy my real passion.

Duke, Alexa and Stacy headed toward the beach to get a closer look, but Abby and Skipper stayed in the Winnebago, presumably to continue chronicling our trip. At least I think Abby was doing that. Skip was probably just yawning and scratching his...er....ears.

Apparently, Roger had alerted the local newspaper and soon a young woman appeared before our rolling circus, note pad and pen in hand. She was probably 25 years old, brunette.... cute. I know that has absolutely nothing to do with our story but, hey, I'm young and single at this point.

"Is there a Corky here?" the young lady asked.

"Yep, I'm Corky," I responded in my most authoritative voice, which wasn't much.

"So, I understand you're from California. What made you want to surf here at our little beach?" the girl asked.

"Well first of all, what's your name," I asked the obvious question.

"Oh sorry, Suzy Mayne, *Jacksonville Star*," she replied.

Suzy was about 5'2" inches tall I figured and dressed in cutoff jeans and a tank top. Odd outfit for a reporter I thought. But then the 60s were funny that way.

"Well Suzy my mantra is "all surf is good surf."

"I guess that's a healthy attitude," Suzy said, "Have you surfed pretty much around the world?"

"Not really, although I'd like to," I replied. "My background is mostly Hawaii and California, but I've been surfing on the east coast for the past year or so."

"What made you decide to design boards?" she continued.

"Ah, that wasn't my idea. You can credit Andy, the owner of Jacks for that. He's a great businessman. I'm just a fair to midlin surfer," I replied trying to give credit where credit was due.

"Is it okay if I speak to the rest of the people in your group for a little more background?" Suzy asked.

"Sure, have at it. But I warn you there is nothing particularly interesting about our group. Just a bunch of surfers, a photographer and a writer. Just your average traveling medicine show," I laughed out loud.

"Well thanks, Corky. I think I can get a small article in the paper," Suzy said.

"Can't hurt."

We shook hands and Suzy wandered off in the direction of the beach. She had one of those walks that caused you to watch her until she was out of sight. Oh well, *I certainly don't need that complication* I thought to myself.

I ran down to the beach to try to catch up with my crew. Things were getting hungry in Jacksonville and I wanted to see what everyone had in mind. We could actually cook in the Winnebago, of course, but our first night on the road felt like a perfect opportunity to have a little kick off celebration with pizza and beer or something equally bad for us.

In looking at the ocean I couldn't help but notice some fairly ominous thunderheads looming just off the coast. That could be good news or bad news. If a storm developed further offshore it could kick up some awesome waves. If it moved inland it could kill the whole event. I knew we'd know by later that evening and we did in spades.

I finally spied the registration area and trotted over to our team.

"What's the story?" I asked Gabe.

"Well we're all registered," he said handing me a sort of bib to be worn during the meet. Number 17. I hated those darned bibs but understood why they were necessary. Most of us guys looked pretty much the same. Shaggy hair. Tanned. Baggie shorts. Must have been a pain for the judges trying to determine who was who as we were all bobbing in and out of the waves.

"Here's the thing, though," Gabe continued, "the weather forecast sucks. There are storms moving in and this thing could be a total washout," he said looking totally dejected.

"I don't think I've ever seen a meet cancelled for rain." I said, looking at the darkening skies. The meet started early the next morning so I was hoping the storm would blow over.

"Well, they're predicting lightening…it's a safety thing," Gabe explained.

*"We shall see,"* I thought to myself.

"Hey guys, let's go catch some dinner. I'm up for pizza or burgers or something," I shared my opinion," But definitely some cold beer."

Luckily, we found an Italian restaurant not too far from the parking area for the meet. It featured lots of creative pizzas and even three versions of vegetarian. Abby was one happy lady to have choices. For me the "meat lovers" looked awfully good but almost any of them would have worked as long as there was cold beer. Gee I sound like a .... what's the word my dad used?....lush?...right?

Nope, I was just a thirsty surfer. Acknowledging my Hawaiian heritage, I actually ordered one of the pizzas with pineapple on top, but still had them include pepperoni. Old habits die hard.

We were sitting there just reminiscing about our travels so far when we started hearing some pretty vicious thunder. The dining room also brightened up considerably when the lightening started. I was dreading the walk back to Winnie. Dread was the right emotion as it turned out.

# Chapter Nine

## Thunder Road

Long story short, the event in Jacksonville was a complete washout. Thunder and lightning getting worse as the day wore one. So, the judges used good sense and canceled the event hoping to have another chance at a competition in the fall. We had several days until the next event in Savannah, but Abby really wanted to spend some time in the area called "old town" up there, so she convinced Duke to venture out and head on up the coast in spite of the storm.

Looking back, I think that was a mistake. We had to pull over several times since visibility was nonexistent. Duke even began to look nervous and he never, never looked nervous. It was about 140 miles from Jacksonville Beach to Savannah and we thought it might take about three hours. It ended up taking nearly five hours and we were all quite frazzled when we arrived. The rain had been so heavy at times that water ran across the road and we had to slow down to a crawl. No matter, we just kept moving. Looking back, it would clearly have been a better decision to pull over for the night even if we had to open up some cans of baked beans each.

We got into Savannah about two in the afternoon. The event was actually about three days later out on Tybee Island but all of us were happy for the break. When the weather lifted the surfers on our team could head over to the island to get in some practice, but right now it was just about hunkering down and waiting out the storm. I have to say this was the roughest weather I'd ever seen short of a hurricane. Just brutal.

By the next morning we were able to leave Winnie and do a little touring. Abby was up and gone very early and, luckily for us, took Skipper with her. The two of them were virtually inseparable. I had noticed that she had been heading off on her own a good bit recently. On her own that is except for the pup. I hoped she wasn't feeling left out because she wasn't a surfer. I don't know if she knew how much she brought to our little band of surf bums. She was the stabilizing factor, even getting by with saying things like *"Do you really need another beer, Corky? You have a meet coming up."* Even my mom didn't get on me like that. Well that's a white lie but it's been a while.

Alexa and Stacy wanted to go shopping. For what I don't know. I never know what girls shop for. Sometimes they come back empty handed but tell us they had a great shopping day. Guys will never admit to getting that logic.

We had all made an agreement the night before that if we were able to get out and explore, we would meet back at that spot at 4 pm the next day. So, Duke, Gabe and I were able take Winnie over to Tybee Island for a look at the surf break. The boards where strapped on the mobile home so we could actually get in a few rides if the surf was up. Believe me, the *surf was up!* The remnants of the storm were still stirring the pot and that was to our advantage. Encouraged, Duke and I pulled our boards down and headed out. The water was really warm, a byproduct of the tropical aspects of the storm I guessed.

Once we were in the water we wanted to stay as long as we possibly could. It was early in the season, of course, so we knew the light wouldn't last too long, so we no sooner ended one ride than we paddled back out to try to catch another one. We were working so hard to get in as many rides as possible during the daylight hours that we were exhausted when we finally collapsed on the beach a few hours later.

"Hey, Corky it's pushing 4 o'clock already, we'd better get back," Duke said.

"Holy crap," Gabe said, "the girls aren't going to be happy if we're too late."

"You worry too much," I assured him but as usual he was right. When we finally pulled into the lot at about 4:30 Abby was the first one to scold us for being late.

"Come on, Abby," I tried to reason with her, "Duke and I needed the practice."

"Well the rest of us need food," she pouted. I hated it when she pouted. I don't know if it annoyed me or if the cuteness of it left me without words. But whatever affect it had, she had the team heading off for dinner shortly thereafter.

Almost everywhere we went we faced a challenge finding a menu that suited the entire team. Abby being a committed vegetarian meant that often we had to ask for special preparation for her even as the rest of us wolfed down pasta, or pizza or some humongous burger. This time our only hope was a fairly new Howard Johnson's restaurant not far from where Winnie was parked. The menu had most of our favorite items but lacked our main staple…beer. Oh well, all in good time I told myself.

We all ordered and settled down for a nice meal and to discuss the upcoming event. Just by way of keeping you informed (you do like staying informed, don't you?) Abby had a meal of green beans and potatoes with some zucchini on the side. Looked yukky to me but she seemed to enjoy it.

We had some time to kill the next morning so I told Gabe we would try to find a shop that could develop his pictures. Gabe was more than a little excited at that prospect. I was really interested to see the ones he took in St. Augustine. He was really hitting his stride as a photographer and as his best friend I wanted to do whatever I could to encourage him.

Not too many camera shops actually had darkrooms in their own buildings, but we managed to find one who did their own work in the old town section of Savannah. Jim, the owner, turned out to be a surfer and promised to have the prints back to us by the following afternoon. You could always count on a fellow surfer.

When Gabe and I got back to Winnie we again found Abby working feverishly on her latest journal. She was so engrossed she even asked me to walk Skipper. She and our little pal were so close I wasn't even sure the pup would do his business with me being the walker. Boy was I wrong. If he wasn't a dog, I would have thought he had been drinking beer all the night before.

That afternoon we again headed over to Tybee Island to register for the meet. Tybee was really a lush and underdeveloped island. Not nearly as commercial as Daytona Beach had become. But there were a small number of restaurants and bars and enough tourists to keep the local economy pretty healthy, I guess.

Like Jacksonville this little competition didn't offer a big payday, but since the island was pretty close to Savannah and even part of Florida and South Carolina it drew a good number of decent surfers. One thing we did notice was the large number of female surfers this particular event attracted. Alexa and Stacy were clearly happy to see that, but the first question they asked was whether the girls competed with the boys or just against each other. They seemed to resent competing only with other female surfers and wanted to prove they could compete with the big boys of the sport.

As luck would have it, they were disappointed to be placed into competition with other girls but got over it and began to take the competition seriously. "Might as well try to win," Alexa said.

Another long story short, win she did. Alexa was the big star of our little tour during this visit to Tybee Island. Duke and I placed well up in the pack after the men's heats, but Alexa just aced it and took top prize among the girls. The surf wasn't so impressive that day, but Alexa had caught nearly a perfect ride. Given her size she was able to tuck inside a nice barrel and ride it in. Photo op to be sure. Stacy did well too but just wasn't the surfer Alexa was.

By the time we were ready to leave Georgia, we had one trophy, orders for two CorkBoards ™, a set of great pictures of St. Augustine and the awesome fort. We scheduled call with Andy the following day to bring him up to date.

I was the next team member to ask for a diversion. We were going to slip up to Charleston for an event later that month, but I wanted to head over to Hilton Head Island again. I couldn't really explain it but that place just seemed like home to me and I wanted to visit it again. Somehow this island was going to factor into my future even though I didn't know how or when. I did know that I wanted to take the team to a place called Dolphin Head and have them take in the sights and sounds of the island.

# Chapter Ten

## A Call to Action

Luckily my team members agreed to our little excursion to Hilton Head. When we arrived we right away found an area designated for visiting trailer parking on the north end of the island where we could spend a few days. One thing that was a little more challenging was finding a pay phone where we could make our call to Andy. Apparently, the founders of the island had laid out some pretty strict standards to be sure that things stayed as they were, with palm trees and evergreens everywhere but not many businesses visible from the little road that crossed the island. Shopping was limited, with the island residents heading to the mainland for most of their needs.

We finally found a pay phone at a little shopping center called Coligny Plaza, all the way on the other end of the island. There might have been more but you sure couldn't see them from the road. We had to place the call collect, of course, but Andy anticipated that and took the call immediately.

We really had a lot to tell Andy this time. Our trip so far had not only been successful, in that we got one first place finish, but from an educational standpoint as well. We'd even sold a couple of boards. That fact alone made us feel good about the possibility of selling more CorkBoards (TM) and Jacks products along the way. Of course, that was music to Andy's ears.

During the call I told Andy about the visit to Castillo and the fact that Abby and Gabe had chronicled that visit. I could tell someone was with Andy during the call as he kept repeating what I was telling him. Turned out to be Roger, the young businessman who helped launch the tour. After talking for a while Andy asked me to hang on for a minute.

He finally came back to the phone and said, "Corky, Roger wants you guys to send him the story of the visit to St. Augustine along with the pictures. He thinks they may be of interest to the local paper, assuming of course the material is as good as you say."

"Oh yeah…. it's good stuff," I responded. Both my team members were just damned good at what they did. I told Abby and Gabe what Roger had suggested and they agreed right away.

I gave Andy the details of the first two orders and told him we would put the checks in the mail so he could get started. It was going to cost a fortune to ship the boards to the buyers, but they didn't seem to mind. They had been pulled into the, what's the word, "mystique" of the brand, I guess.

When the call was over everyone was energized, but particularly our two "reporters". We would all be mighty proud if the article and the pictures were published in the News Journal.

We planned to be on the island for about five days at most but wanted to take care of business before having any fun. We found the post office without much trouble and put the orders (with specifications), the checks, photos and Abby's journal, at least the part about the visit to the fort, into the mail. With time on our hands we headed to the beach for a little relaxation. We didn't often just hang out at the beach, no matter where we were.

There was almost always some surfing. This time, however, everyone just wanted to bask in the beautiful sunshine. The weather was almost perfect. The temperature was right at 80 degrees and the humidity low. If we had been determined to surf it wouldn't have been a great day to do it. The ocean was glassy with only the smallest waves breaking on the beach. That reality more or less gave us permission to take the day off and just vegetate on the sand.

As we lay side by side on the beach we began to talk about the prospect of Abby and Gabe being published in the Daytona paper.

"I wonder what the angle would be for the article?" Duke asked.

"I think they would use it to talk about Florida history," Stacy suggested.

Gabe scratched his head and wondered out loud, "Maybe we should have some sort of paper that says what we write, or my pictures actually belong to us."

"I understand what you mean," I said, "But, if Andy trusts Roger, I guess we should too. I mean he got the tour off and running and didn't really ask for anything in return."

"Well I'm sure he has some sort of deal worked out with Andy," Abby said.

We all lay there silent for a while until Duke finally blurted out the obvious "I guess we'll find out pretty soon."

That evening we had dinner inside the Winnebago with the ladies volunteering to whip up a special treat. The treat ended up being veggie lasagna and red beans. Now I'm not a vegetarian by a long shot but that meal just hit the spot. Abby was really happy of course and thanked everyone for going along with a meatless meal. At least we found something we all enjoyed. It wouldn't be the last time we had that meal.

The next day we again went our own ways. Alexa and Stacy headed on up the coast to a little water town called Beaufort and convinced Abby to tag along. Like so many southern towns it had a history and was really "charming" to quote the brochures. Duke wanted to find some sort of sailing excursion. Gabe was going to walk the beaches looking for good shots, but he and I agreed to reconnect later in the day at the trailer parking area. I headed directly for Dolphin Head with the goal of just re-energizing.

A guy I had met on my first visit to the island had clued me in about the little beach on Port Royal Sound. He insisted that it was a very special place...a place of relaxation and reflection. He wasn't wrong. There was no surf at Dolphin Head, but then maybe that was part of the draw for me. Like our day at the beach where there was no break, there was also nothing to distract me from my thoughts. Every once in a while, I think everyone needs that. Sorry for getting philosophical. It happens sometimes (but not too often so don't get used to it).

I guess the only thing that might have ruined my day was spotting my first alligator. It was sunning at the edge of a little lagoon I encountered walking down to the beach. He looked like he might be about six or seven feet long and lay there with his mouth wide open. I wasn't about to provide the filler he was looking for and quietly walked away. I later found out that they were pretty laid back and were really nothing to worry about, but my first encounter was, I have to admit, surprising.

I stayed on Dolphin Head for most of the rest of that day, only heading back to meet the others when hunger overtook my quest for peace and quiet. I was quite a way from Winnie and, as I had done earlier in the day, I flagged a ride up route 278 back to the far northern end of the island. The guy who picked me up was a local and quite amused by my look.

My hair had gotten pretty long, down to my shoulders in fact. I seldom wore shoes, mostly just sandals. Of course, most of my time was spent in warm climates so shorts and t-shirts were my standard outfit.

The driver of the car had on coveralls and a baseball cap. His standard outfit as well I guessed. He told me he worked on furnaces and air conditioners. Had his own business. He let me know that there wasn't much call for furnace repair, but air conditioners kept him pretty busy year-round. I suppose I didn't need to know that, but I didn't mind listening to him talk. He seemed like a nice enough guy. He was pretty close to my age, so I decided to ask his advice on restaurants on the island. He directed me to a diner on the main road. Said the meatloaf was, his words, "to die for". I didn't have the heart to tell him we had a committed vegetarian in our group. Somehow, I thought that might offend him.

"I never met a real hippie," my chauffer said. His name turned out to be Pete. He asked mine and he looked at me a little oddly when I told him it was Corky.

"Well, I'm not a hippie, Pete, just a surfer."

"Really?" Pete said, "Never really knew one of those either. Happy to meet you".

"You too, Pete, and I really appreciate the ride."

"No sweat…uh…Corky," Pete said still trying to wrap his head around my nickname I guessed.

"So, Pete, do you actually live on the island," I asked.

"Born and bred. Got no reason to move to the mainland. My folks were born here, and our kin go all the way back to the civil war. Kinda proud of that," Pete beamed.

"I'll bet you are. Not much around here, though. Don't you miss the stores and bars and those types of things on the mainland?" I was growing fascinated with this young guy.

"Naw, anyway I don't drink much. Just a brew with my buddies once in a while. And what would I shop for? I'm not married…don't even have a girl right now. Maybe someday," Pete didn't seem to mind my questions.

"Well I sure love your island, Pete. I can see why you would hate to leave it," I said sincerely, "In fact I could see settling down here someday. But likely I'll head back to Cali sometime."

"Cali?" Pete looked confused.

"Oh, sorry, I mean California where I'm from," I replied.

"Kinda figured."

Soon Pete had me to the entrance of the parking area and stuck out his hand," If you ever want to tour the island, I'm pretty good at telling all about it. There's really no place like it."

"I may just take you up on that, Pete, but how would I get in touch with you?" I responded, not actually thinking I would ever see him again.

Pete reached into his coveralls and pulled out a wrinkled business card and handed it to me. On the card it said, "Pete's Heating and Air" and had the saying "We Care About Your Air" along with his phone number.

We shook hands and Pete said, "Ya'll come back now, hear?" he looked embarrassed even as he said it. "…. dang sorry about that, I heard it on a TV show". We both laughed and Pete soon disappeared beyond a stand of live Oak trees.

By the time I got back to Winnie, the whole group was there and sitting in a circle outside the van swapping stories about their adventures that day. As usual the girls talked about the little shops in Beaufort. Duke on the other hand had found a boat excursion that took him around Hilton Head and even to another nearby island with virtually no inhabitants called Daufuskie. He was genuinely impressed and insisted we should all try it if we had time. I made a note to myself to find out more.

I filled the team in on my visit to Dolphin Head and told them about hitching a ride with Pete. Thus far in our trip the residents in most of the southern towns had turned out to be more hospitable than we imagined, and Pete was no exception. In fact, I often thought about Sheriff Girth and his sister **in** Louisiana. These folks sure weren't what we were told to expect.

After a while Abby grew sort of philosophical and wondered out loud what we all might be doing if it weren't for our little surfing adventure and how long it might last.

Duke was the first one to respond and said he most definitely would not be selling furniture at his dad's store in Ormond Beach and didn't want to end up managing it until he retired "or died". He clearly didn't really know what he wanted to do with his life. I had found that out when I first met him on the beach that day, but hey, we were still young and had some time to plan.

Gabe mentioned he might like to make photography his full-time career. That came as no surprise of course. It was also no revelation that Abby wanted to write full time.

When it came to me, I actually surprised myself. "If I couldn't surf and had to choose, I might start a little restaurant or bar somewhere warm, maybe even someplace like this. A tiki bar or something might be cool." The only thing that I could figure brought that to mind was Abby's uncle's place in Half Moon Bay, California. Her uncle Ben Colter just seemed like he enjoyed cooking up comfort food and serving folks in that quaint little town. Of course, he did have a soft spot for the surfing crowd.

Yep, maybe that's what made me blurt that out. Abby was just nodding her head as I mentioned it. Seemed like somehow, she knew.

# Chapter Eleven

## A Bit of Good News and The Road Ahead

Before we knew it a couple of days had passed, and it was time to call Andy again. Of course, we didn't have much to report this time, but boy did he have some news.

After the usual greetings, Andy excitedly told us about how the story and pictures we had submitted were received by the paper. "To put it mildly, they loved the whole thing. They said the writing was first class and pictures…. let's see…what was the word they used….uh… "elegant".

Gabe seemed to blush at that word, "Hey guys I'm elegant," he said chuckling.

"No partner, not you…your pictures," I shot back.

"So, what does all that mean, Andy?" Abby asked.

"Well here's the deal," Andy continued, "They want you to keep writing and taking photos as the tour keeps moving and send them in regularly. They think the readers will eat it up. Summer adventures and all that. In return they're going to pay you a little bit for each article and even cut me a break on ads for Jack's in the paper."

"How much?" Gabe asked without hesitation.

"50 bucks each," Andy responded, "Not too bad for doing what you love doing anyway, eh?"

"We'll take it!" Abby said, smiling broadly, "My first paid gig...what do you think about that?".

The news from Daytona was just the boost our team needed. The CorkBoards ™ tour was actually getting press coverage. It didn't seem possible.

Our visit to Hilton Head was almost over and we knew we had to head on up to Charleston. Before we went, though, I felt like I had one little loop to close. For some reason I kept thinking Pete, my air conditioning repairman/chauffer had been trying to make a new friend. I decided to call him before leaving the island.

I got him right away. "Hey, Pete, Corky. Do you remember me?" I said.

"Sure, man, how you doin?" Pete actually seemed glad to hear from me.

"Hangin in there," I said, "I just wanted you to know that we're leaving the island, but I'd like a raincheck on that tour if that's cool."

"No problem, hippie, next time through I'll give you that grand tour and we maybe we can have a brew."

"Again, Pete, not a hippie...but you're on...I'll call you in a few weeks."

"Talk then, man," Pete said apparently trying to sound hip.

As soon as everyone was packed up and ready, we headed back out onto the highway shooting for a place called Isle of Palms. It was Charleston, South Carolina's beach community and host to a couple of small surfing competitions each year. Even so, we were kind of clueless as to what sort of action we might find.

As luck would have it, we had a flat tire on our way to our destination. A flat tire on a Winnebago? Not something you planned for or knew right away how to handle. Duke and Gabe hopped out of Winnie and stood looking at the pitiful tire. It was flatter than a flitter. I have to admit I never knew what a flitter was. Guess I'll have to look that up someday. (Authors note: Corky never did look it up, but I did. It's a misappropriation of the word fritter...which is flat...you owe me).

Good news was that the monstrous van came with a manual and a spare tire. Seems as though the manufacturer anticipated the occasional blowout and decided to provide instructions on how to deal with it. Good thing because just finding the jack was a challenge. Anyway, Duke and Gabe put some muscle to it and soon we were back on the road. Both my buddies congratulated me on being a good supervisor.

When we got to Isle of Palms a few hours later we found a parking spot near the beach and decided to settle down for the night. I was surprised that Gabe volunteered to try to cook us up a little dinner. That was the good news. The bad news was that it was basically packaged macaroni and cheese. Now I always loved that food group, but Gabe managed to serve up a soggy variation alongside a garden salad that really should have stayed in the garden. No matter everyone ate a plateful and thanked him for his efforts.

The event at Isle of Palms turned out to be a pretty minor meet with no serious prize money. The most important things we got out of that stop were some pretty nice pictures and a story Abby wrote about the efforts of the locals to preserve the beach area and prevent over commercialization.

Much of the rest of our first month on the road was like that. There were a million small beach towns with simple surf competitions and many others with nothing going on. No matter, there were tourists everywhere and our little road show took people by surprise. We soon realized that we could draw attention to ourselves and therefore CorkBoards ™ and Jacks by simply camping out near the ocean and having Duke crank up the music. That would normally draw at least a small crowd. We got pretty good at spinning the story of our quest to surf as many events as possible and Abby was able to interview locals about subjects as different as local cooking and other local preservation efforts. Occasionally we would run into surfers from the area and, even though Abby's interest in surfing had sort of faded, she interviewed them anyway and some good stories came of those interviews. The surfers loved being interviewed by the cute little redhead and we made some new friends as we surfed our way north.

And speaking of friends, when we got to Virginia Beach, we were reunited with some surfers we had met the year before during the East Coast Surfing Championship. Everyone was pretty excited because some big names were headed into town to compete, not the least of which was Corky Carroll from California. He had placed second last year and I felt certain he would really go for it this year. One of the highlights of last season had been meeting the "real" Corky and talking with him even if only briefly. I thought he was a good guy even though he was considered one of the real stars of surfing. He could have been full of himself, but he didn't come off that way at all.

Imagine my surprise when we crossed paths again during registration and he actually remembered me.

"So, what's with the CorkBoards ™ deal," Corky Carroll asked. I explained how it all came together and he seemed genuinely impressed. I kind of knew that was about the only way I would impress him that day. As I'm sure you guessed, he went on to win the 1968 event. His rides were spectacular by east coast standards.

After the event I worked my way through the crowd and found Corky again, congratulated him and invited him to come down to Daytona if he had the time.

"I'm headed back to California right away," Corky said, "I want to finish the season with as many wins as I can," he explained. Corky had always been a real model for how surfers represented the sport and made their way through a tricky world of competitive surfing. He knew that I was also from California and suggested I stop by his place in Huntington Beach when I got back. I told him I would, but I wasn't at all sure I would even go back. The east coast has its own appeal and I was beginning to feel at home. I guess I'll talk more about that later.

Corky and I shook hands and pledged to stay in touch, but I knew he was one busy guy, so I didn't get my hopes up.

Duke actually did really well in this year's east coast meet and the local press ate up the story of our little quest. Duke was good at talking to fans and the press and made the most of his moment in the sun. He even signed some autographs. It was actually pretty difficult to pull him away from the group of admirers that seemed to follow him around. But we finally had to move on.

Our trek continued up the east coast and I have to say that the weather contributed to our success most places we visited. Mid 70s to mid-80s and manageable humidity for several weeks in a row. Whether we surfed competitively or not, we continued to attract attention and even managed to take some orders. During our periodic calls with Andy he made it clear how happy he was with the results. That made it all seem worth it.

Onward.

# Chapter Twelve

## Alexa and A Legendary Character

I'm really embarrassed to admit this, but even though I grew up in Hawaii I had no idea that the island used to be called the "Sandwich Islands". Gabe knew I guess but he tried to tell me they were named after a softshell crab sandwich. Boloney of course. No, not a bologna sandwich…come on, you know what I meant.

I had to look it up, but the real truth is that they were named after a dude called John Montagu. He was called the 4th Earl of Sandwich, First Lord of the Admiralty. Quite a mouthful. I promise the significance of the name of the islands will be revealed soon.

I found out that the only grain of truth in Gabe's version of the story was that old John invented the sandwich. Well actually his butler did. Seems like John liked to gamble and didn't want to even take a break for a meal. So, he asked his butler to create something he could hold in his hand and still place bets. The butler put some meat between two slices of bread and so it began. Or so they say. Whoever "they" are.

Enough history, back to surfing.

You may have noticed that Alexa and Stacy had been pretty quiet, except for shopping trips. Good reason for that.

Alexa was really focused on getting back up to New England and competing in some of her favorite surfing events. She had made us promise to get her there in time to be a part of things.

One stop we knew we had to make on our trip was Asbury Park in New Jersey. That was where Alexa's great, great, great grandmother was supposed to have done the first surfing on the east coast. Her real name isn't known but they call her the Sandwich Island Girl and Alexa swears to be a direct descendant. (See I told you I would let you know why I mentioned the Sandwich Islands.

Alexa told us that on August 18, 1888 a drawing of her on her board appeared on the cover of the National Police Gazette and set off a long process of trying to identify her. Whether the story was true or not a lot of people in North Carolina were eager to prove it a fake since they claim the first real surfing on the east coast happened at Wrightsville Beach. Alexa later told me her folks had told her that the story of her ancestor had been passed down through each generation and she was convinced it was true. It also meant that Alexa may have had some Hawaiian roots back there somewhere. Dunno, but it sure made for great conversation.

Just to be clear, as for surfing skills, I think from a style standpoint Alexa may have always been the best of our bunch. I just think she had complete control of her body and that's real advantage when the waves get unpredictable. It was a gas to watch her surf for many reasons.

Actually, I kind of hoped the Sandwich Island Girl story was true. I was beginning to think like a capitalist and thought it would be good for business if it was. I actually said *"shame on you"* in my mind but I guess time was catching up with me and money began to be a factor in my decision-making process.

Andy would probably be happy to know that. I decided to let him in on the story on the next call.

Of course, Alexa allowing us to capitalize on the legend was another matter. I thought it might be a good idea to discuss it with her first. I decided to try to cut her from the pack when we pulled over for the night.

That day we ended up in a little town outside of Baltimore with no particular design on surfing the area, just getting a decent night's sleep. By late the next day we would be entering New England and beginning to live out Alexa's dream. Can't say it wasn't sort of intriguing. Her background was so different from mine (unless you count the possible Hawaiian link) that every story she told seemed a bit exotic.

I more or less engineered the opportunity to talk with her one on one by asking her if she wanted to walk off a relatively heavy dinner of Maryland seafood. The worst or best part of the meal, depending upon your outlook, were the hush puppies. I ask you, who came up with that belly buster? Even though you knew they were a heart attack waiting to happen they were absolutely irresistible.

It was a really pretty evening with a light breeze and a temperature of around 75 degrees, the kind of evening that made you feel alive.

"Lex…I want to run something by you," I opened up.

"Corky I thought we covered all of that," she sniffed, I gathered referring to my amateurish romantic overtures. Okay…guilty as charged.

"No, no…not that," I quickly cut her off.

"Okay, shoot."

"The stories you tell about the Sandwich Island Girl, your family really thinks all of that is true right?" I started carefully.

"It is true," Alexa said without hesitation.

"Well okay, then. Why haven't you been letting folks know that the legend lives on…through you?"

"Huh?"

"There aren't too many really cool stories that involve surfing history, much less the surfing heroes like your ancestor…see my meaning?"

"Well yes," Alexa replied," But local papers ran articles about it back then…they just didn't convince people that she was real."

"Well then, suppose we take up that cause and *make* her real to all the surfers on the east coast who want to believe in our sport. I mean…we need our heroes just like the original Duke, Duke Kahanamoku out in Hawaii, "I said finding myself preaching rather than suggesting, "I mean I grew up idolizing that guy."

"Your point? What are you asking?" Alexa had that stubborn look on her face.

"Okay, here goes. I think we should promote you as the direct descendent of the Sandwich Island Girl. It will draw crowds, sell surfboards and allow Abby and Gabe to promote great stories to the Florida papers. Heck they might even get picked up nationally."

"So, what's the catch?" Alexa asked as anticipated.

"Well, I mean you have to actually *live* the part of her great, great, great….whatsit," I tried to explain, "In other words you not only have to believe it you have to know the story and tell it well."

"But I believe it's real."

"Exactly...but you have to be willing to convince others it's real...ya know?" I preached on.

"I think I get it. You want to use my family to make money. Am I close," Alexa was now growing a little testy.

"Um...yes...but no...but...if it's a true story all you are doing is telling the world about it and promoting yourself as a surfer as a byproduct. I mean you're one of the best I ever saw," I said being very careful not to mention that she was a girl. Very careful.

Alexa sighed and looked away. I could tell she was in deep thought.

"I can't say I haven't tried to tell the story before," Alexa offered up, "Just never could find anybody that seemed interested."

"So, will you at least think it over and we can discuss it more in the next few days?" I ventured.

"Okay. that much I can do."

"I mean, we should really think it through before you start competing in New England...it could be big," I pointed out.

"Granted," Alexa conceded.

"Did you ever hear why the Sandwich Islands were named that?" I asked.

"Don't care," Alexa resumed the Alexa persona.

"Okay, then," I concluded the talk.

The next day I was more than a little surprised when Alexa came to the back of Winnie as we tooled up the highway and said, "Let's do this."

I was mighty tempted to make an off-color joke at that moment but new immediately that would be a big ass mistake.

To accommodate Alexa, we had decided that our next stop would be Newport, Rhode Island. Alexa told us there were surf competitions throughout the summer in that immediate area and we figured her hometown would be a great home base. By staying in touch with friends in Rhode Island she knew that there would be events in Little Compton, and Matunuck. But her favorite spot and one where there was a significant competition that summer was Narraganset.

"With just the right weather the breaks can be impressive," she assured us. It seems she had a pretty well-established reputation in Rhode Island and some other parts of the New England states, so returning there would be a treat for her and for all of our troop, that matter.

In Newport we were able to find a sign maker who could quickly fashion a sign based on Stacy's design that announced, *"The Return of the Sandwich Island Girl"*. Stretching the truth a bit, but good promo anyhow. Duke managed to find a way to fasten it to the front of Winnie so that it was the first thing you saw when we pulled into our destination.

Now we had even more to talk about with the locals. Abby and Gabe were, needless to say, very happy about the Sandwich Island development and planned at least two articles with pictures covering Alexa's adventures in New England. Andy was also happy with this turn of events and told us he would alert the Daytona paper about the stories to come. I only hoped there was a story to tell.

I shouldn't have worried. Right away Alexa directed us to a spot in Narraganset where surfers tended to hang out and where the break was fairly reliable if not spectacular every day. The first thing I noticed was that all of the surfers on the beach that day seemed to know both Alexa and Stacy. There were lots of hugs and kisses and more than a few high fives.

The second thing I noticed was that the surfers in that part of the country looked a lot more like hippies than I was used to. By this time, most of us guys had longish hair but nothing like the guys we were seeing. Many had hair long enough to pull it back in ponytails. Some had fairly significant beards. The girls all seemed to be wearing beads and peace sign necklaces…at least when they weren't surfing. It seemed like a clash of cultures to me, but Gabe had a field day snapping pictures and Alexa was clearly in her element.

Once the initial greetings were finished, Alexa walked over toward me with what I guessed was a local surfer.

"Corky I'd like for you to meet my cousin Frankie," Alexa said.

"Frankie De Silva," the young guy said, sticking out his hand. Frankie was about 6'3" and sported a great tan. His hair was to his shoulders…about like mine, I guess. He looked a bit Spanish to me but what do I know. My name is Spanish and I'm not. Go figure.

"Corky Sandoval," I said offering up the brother shake.

"I hear you're a pretty darn good surfer, Corky," Frankie said.

"I've always said I may not be great, but I'm committed," I repeated my mantra laughing.

"Well my cousin here is the real deal, even if she is a girl." Alexa immediately punched Frankie's shoulder.

"It's a good thing you're her cousin. I can't get by with that line," I stated the obvious.

"Frankie has won some awards around this area and actually competed down at Virginia Beach a couple of years ago," Alexa said.

"Well I look forward to seeing what you can do, Frankie."

"Me too. Anyway, welcome to this neck of the woods," Frankie said again shaking my hand. "I'll catch up with you two later. I have to meet some guys to barter a couple of boards."

We spent the rest of that day catching as many waves as we could. Traveling in the Winnebago was comfortable but tedious and surfing loosened us up after miles on the road. Alexa and Stacy ended up getting the best rides of the day. I supposed that was because they knew the area well and could read the water. That was a phrase I had picked up from a young friend in Galveston, Texas. Joey always told me "you can catch a wave at any beach in the world if you learn to read the water."

Smart young dude. I hoped he was doing well.

As the sun got lower in the sky we decided to head back to Newport for some dinner and a meeting to formulate our plans for this part of the trip. When we were on Hilton Head Island, we had come to like a native southern meal called shrimp and grits. After eating it at a little roadside diner we asked around and found that it had been a staple during a time when slaves lived in that area. The Gullah people perfected it and eventually it caught on with others in the Lowcountry.

So, Abby volunteered to fix that for dinner along with some collard greens. The only catch was that the grits, or at least some of them, had to be cooked separately and the greens couldn't be cooked in bacon drippings like they often did in the south. Oh well. Worth a try.

I have to give Abby come credit. The meal tasted great.

During our dinner meeting Alexa laid out plans for us to compete in an event at Little Compton in three days and then head back to Narragansett for a more competitive meet there about a week later. It would mean generally staying put for a few days but, after all, we were there to surf. Next Alexa convinced us that we might want to head to Massachusetts for a few days and then double back to Asbury Park, New Jersey where the original Sandwich Island Girl had reportedly surfed in 1888.

That all sounded good and, as we finished our meals, we all toasted the *new* Sandwich Island Girl and pledged to move on. Skipper snored on the floor.

# Chapter Thirteen

## Read the Water and Catch a Break

I was amazed at how many people in New England knew the story of the Sandwich Island Girl. People were constantly pulling us aside and asking what was up with the sign. Seems like a lot of surfers held "ole Sandwich" as a hero in that area. Alexa got pretty good at spinning tales of her ancestor and her exploits on her makeshift board. I came to find out that her family had done a fair amount of research on the story and Alexa quickly became the family historian as it related to the legend.

The competition at Little Compton lived up to the "little" part of the name. Little to no surf that particular day. The weather was nice but actually too nice. It was sunny but the wind was calm, almost dead still. Some waves were running not much more than a foot. I noticed that you might see a pretty nice swell and think something big was coming but that they sometimes didn't crest at all.

Duke and I decided not to surf in that event. It just didn't seem worth the effort. Alexa and Stacy on the other hand were chomping at the bits to get into the water. Alexa was clearly an expert at reading the water as my young friend called it and caught everything worth catching. I couldn't figure out how she could pick her rides with such accuracy and she wasn't about to tell me. Stacy was almost as good.

At this event there was a guys' division and a girls' division. That didn't make Alexa happy, but she decided to make the most of it and went on to win her division with ease. Stacy placed 4th but was happy with her day given the tiny break.

There was a master of ceremonies of sorts with a way too loud public address system who kept interrupting the action with his commentary. He looked like a local college kid but, man, did he take his job seriously. Anyway, he did us a bit of a service when he announced that Alexa won her heat by calling her "the new Sandwich Island Girl". Her win and the acknowledgement from College Joe caused people to flock over to Winnie to talk surfing and sometimes place orders. I was really grateful that Alexa posed for pictures with a Corkboard, the logo clearly visible. In fact, several people in the crowd were taking pictures and Gabe told me later he got some good shots that should make Andy really happy.

All in all, a pretty good day despite pretty crappy surf. On to Narraganset.

By the time the Narraganset event rolled around the weather had changed radically. There was a modest Nor'easter off the coast and the waves were running 5 to 7 feet. Impressive enough for a fairly good ride.

All four of us registered for the event. Looking around, Duke and I felt pretty confident going into this competition. Some of the local guys looked like they had been up all night. Duke and I were young, healthy guys, of course, but were also determined to stay healthy. So, we actually got a good night's sleep before we competed. I was hoping that would pay off.

I wish I could tell you we "ran the board" but it's as if the wheels fell off for our crew. Only Stacy had any kind of showing, her placement not worth mentioning. That day the crowds flocked around not us but Alexa's cousin Frankie. He ran away with the event and had some of the prettiest rides I've ever seen. Frankie was just like Alexa in that he had full command of his body. He could also read the water with the best of them. I was more than a little impressed.

We made a point of congratulating him and then basically limped out of town "thus chastened" as my dad used to say. After we were on the road for a while Alexa came to me and handed me an order for a Corkboard and the payment. I was surprised and very happy to find it came from Frankie. Good guy even if he did kick my butt.

We decided to head on up to Massachusetts to an area around New Bedford, not far from the true cape, where a small annual event was scheduled a few days later. In a little-known cove called "Pocket Beach" local surfers had found that a peculiar reef formation made for a very interesting break. It was a bit dangerous as there were rocks to be dealt with, but if you were relatively experienced you could navigate the hazards.

New Bedford being a very historic whaling and seafaring town we thought we might soak up some culture. We headed to the waterfront that was literally part of the downtown area and were blown away by the activity on the water. The town was pretty industrial, and you had to be impressed with all the work being done on the fishing boats. Some people talked about the smell of the fishing industry and how offensive it could be, but to me it represented the ocean and nothing about the ocean could ever be offensive to me.

We all commented to Abby that it was a shame she was a vegetarian since we all planned to have a nice seafood meal while we were in town. She responded with a look of revulsion. Girl didn't know what she was missing. At a little bar near the wharf called Eddie's, that evening I had the best crab legs I think I ever had...and that time I didn't even notice what Abby ate.

There was a little band playing on a tiny stage at the bar. Their songs were mostly British invasion things, Stones, Yardbirds and so forth. Color me surprised when Duke walked up at break and asked if he could sit in on guitar. I know no one in our group had any idea he could play at all, but he turned out to be darned good. He started off the distinctive riff to the Stones song "Last Time" and the band jumped in as if they had all played together for years. Duke even sang some backup vocals. After that song finished the guys in the band tried to convince him to sit in for a while longer but he left the stage after a few high fives and rejoined our table.

"Damn, brother, you rock!" Gabe said. Everyone slapped Duke on the back and congratulated him. He seemed really embarrassed but I knew he loved the attention.

The Pocket Beach event the next day was a great deal of fun. The break was just as strange as they said we might expect and really challenging. We all managed to at least finish the event and make some friends, but no prize money was being handed out. Not even a trophy. All four of us had good rides but we quickly found out that very little judging was going on except by the small but enthusiastic crowd who rated the ride by their applause. Oh well, it all counts in the whole plan of things.

Our next stop was further south and one that Alexa had made us all look forward to. Asbury Park, New Jersey. Home of the Sandwich Island Girl. Town of many distractions and temptations we were told. There was no competition scheduled there either but based on what Alexa told us, the surfing would be top notch and our exposure to surfing fans widespread. It was after all the peak of tourist season.

Gabe was immediately taken by the boardwalk, much like he had been at Daytona Beach. He headed off to explore right way. Abby decided to hang out with Alexa and Stacy and try to gather some "color" about Alexa's great, great, great grandmother (no idea how many greats there might have been...sorry).

Duke and I pulled our boards down and headed off to the water. Abby, Alexa and Stacy sat on down on the beach for a chat that would form the basis for part of Abby's latest story for the paper.

*"My friend Alexa De Silva is being called the "new" Sandwich Island Girl. If you've never heard of the original Sandwich Island Girl, then you must not be a student of surfing. Purportedly this legendary woman was the first person to introduce surfing to the United States, predating Duke Kahanamoku by at least two years. People first spotted her surfing at Asbury Park, New Jersey in 1888 and a story appeared in the Police Gazette, with a cover picture of a woman in the full swim dress of the time, apparently surfing on a flat almost rectangular "surfboard".*

*The story goes that she learned the sport in Hawaii where she grew up. You may remember that Hawaii used to be called the Sandwich Islands. Thus, the name. She was supposed to be the daughter of an enormously rich planter. She came to the US in the company of a New York importer and caused quite a stir* with the young men in Manhattan society. She was noted as a great dancer and swimmer. Most thought her to be well educated and accomplished. Interesting to note that she was reported to have a fine British accent. And she was very athletic, of course. She once told some admirers that where she came from "girls learn swimming as a matter of course quite as much as girls in this country learn tennis and croquet."

Alexa says she is a direct descendent and her family backs her up on that claim. Ironically (or not) she is an accomplished surfer winning many competitions on the east coast."

There was more to Abby's story of course. She filled in the blanks about our travels and how we headed for New England in search of Alexa's background. It was a really good story and Gabe was able to take some nice shots of the place where the original Sandwich Island Girl is said to have started the whole craze. He also captured Alexa looking very proud to carry on the tradition.

We ended up staying in Asbury Park for a while, surfing, looking for more clues about the legendary Sandwich Island Girl and in general enjoying long summer days together. Soon enough we would head south again and spend the rest of the summer telling tall tales and riding tall waves. Life was good.

Surf's up!

# Chapter Fourteen

## Coda (or not)

It was September 4 when we arrived back in Daytona Beach. We had stayed in touch with Andy all along the way and he knew when to expect our arrival. We had no idea to anticipate a welcoming party and by that time were so road weary we weren't certain we wanted one.

None-the-less as we pulled up to the shop there stood Andy surrounded by several local surfers, tourists and even a reporter from the Daytona paper with his own photographer. As we stepped out of Winnie the small crowd burst into applause and a few whistles. I noticed that Abby was blushing, which looked even more strange on a redhead.

The welcome looked really nice but at that moment I wondered if we had accomplished very much. We hadn't won any major competitions, but we had been written up by the local press from time to time. We did sell some CorkBoards ™ and other Jack's merchandise. We had met the Sandwich Island Girl...more or less...and now were true believers. Most important I think, we had become a real team. I guess the trip had been a success.

Andy came rushing forward and hugged each one of us. He was beaming. It made me feel good that he was. Andy made our summer really remarkable and I don't think any of us will ever be able to forget our adventures or maybe ever top them. I looked back on my doubts about staying and working at the shop and realized that none of this could have happened if I'd headed back to Cali right away. Duke might have been selling furniture all summer (although I kind of doubted it), Abby might have hitchhiked right out of our lives, along with our pal Skipper, and the two New England girls would no doubt have headed north, maybe for good. Gabe and I would likely have been back on the road and looking for some illusive dream. So, it worked out. So far.

In Virginia Beach I remembered talking with Corky Carroll about visiting him in Huntington Beach and doubting that I would ever head west again. I was no further along in my thinking as I stood looking at my large group of east coast friends that day. I had taken on a new life and one I never expected to happen. I decided thinking about it any further could wait a few more days while we all basked in our success. Yep…that's the ticket…take a little break. The answer would come.

# Chapter Fifteen

## A New Beginning

Greg Priestly sat at his desk at his office in Virginia Beach looking at a map of the eastern United States. The map was well worn and had notes and markings all over it. It looked almost like a treasure map. Maybe it would turn out to be one.

Greg felt as though he now had a better understanding of this Corky fellow. He knew that Corky had to be one of the good guys. In addition to being a somewhat accomplished surfer, he needed to be a leader of sorts. Now that a clearer picture was emerging, Greg felt like he could let his mind wander towards preparing for the move and planning the beach bar he had always envisioned. Of course, he had to decide where he wanted to move. Making the right decision would no doubt help keep Lee onboard.

After a while his administrative assistant came in to remind him of his 11am appointment with a client from Williamsburg. Greg was beginning to dread these sorts of meetings, but this man ran a pretty large company serving the military and the account generated a good bit of cash for the firm. He thanked his assistant and asked her to put the client in the conference room and he'd be in in just a minute.

He knew he couldn't dodge this meeting. Greg's client, Walt McKittrick, was considering purchasing another company and Greg knew he planned to bring along his attorney to discuss the transaction. As he entered the conference room and extended his hand to Walt, Greg was taken aback to see JR standing there.

"Greg Priestly, I'd like for you to meet my attorney JR Richfield," Walt said.

Greg and JR shook hands. Clearly JR was as surprised as Greg, but they exchanged pleasantries.

"Fully disclosing, Walt, Greg and I have worked together once before. I don't see a conflict but thought you should know."

"What kind of deal was it?" Walt asked.

"Just a start up that really never got off the ground," Greg explained. He knew that JR knew he was planning to move on to a new life but didn't want Walt to know. At least not yet.

"Well I don't see a problem," Walt assured them. "Just strengthens the team I think."

The three got down to the business at hand. After about half an hour Walt's cell phone rang and he asked to be excused so that he could take the call in the lobby. Once alone, JR and Greg could speak freely.

"What a shock to walk in and see you," Greg admitted.

"Walt never told me your name, so I didn't have any idea," JR explained.

"Well no harm. My clients just haven't been told yet and may not be until I sell the practice," Greg said pushing back in his chair, a little more comfortable now.

"So, where does the plan stand now?" JR asked.

"Still on the drawing board but Lee and I have talked a bit more and I fleshed out the Corky story some," Greg updated his friend.

"Can't wait to hear more of it," JR said as Walt reentered the room.

"Well we might as well end this meeting right now," Walt was fuming. "The other firm is entertaining other offers. I thought this thing was all but done."

Greg could tell Walt was fit to be tied and offered him a drink from his small wet bar. Walt readily accepted. The three men sat sipping straight Knob Creeks silently for more than ten minutes. Eventually Walt stood and exited the room thanking each man for being there and assuring them their fees would be covered in any case. Neither Greg nor JR were worried, but it was nice of Walt to mention it.

After Walt was gone JR continued asking about Greg's plans.

"Right now, I'm just trying to figure out where to plant my new roots," Greg explained. "I want it to be somewhere where Lee feels really comfortable. I think we're a little beyond setting up business where spring breakers congregate. (Authors note: Greg actually hated the word "congregate" because his mom used it to describe how teenagers got together in groups to talk and play music. She was disdainful in using that term he thought.)

"Have you narrowed it down some?" JR asked.

"I think so," Greg said. "I have four places in mind. Isle of Palms near Charleston, South Carolina, Hilton Head Island also off the coast of South Carolina, St. Simons and Tybee Islands off of mainland Georgia. All of them are somewhat gentrified but still have that beach vibe."

"Have you visited each one?"

"Well, no. Only Hilton Head and St. Simons, but I've read a lot about the others," Greg explained.

"Then eliminate them," JR said rather emphatically.

"Huh?"

"Look, Greg, if they weren't worth visiting then I'd say you already have your mind made up. Or at least you're down to those two you've visited. Am I right?"

"Hmmm.... I guess so," Greg admitted.

"Okay, then which one of those last two to you love...I mean where you feel you were meant to be?" JR pressed on.

"You know, JR, I was sitting at a Tiki bar on Hilton Head when I was there on business several years ago and told myself...maybe I should be there. That island just grabbed me at the time. Maybe that was a sign."

"Has Lee been there yet?" JR asked.

"Nope. Unless it was in a former life," Greg chuckled.

"Take her there for a long weekend or whatever. Let her fall in love with it like you did."

Greg thought about that idea for about a minute before saying, "JR you're a brilliant attorney and fair to middlin surfer."

"Well, thanks, I guess," JR laughed out loud. "Hey Greg, can we get out of here and have another drink at your local watering hole, whatever that is?"

"You bet!"

Greg ended up having to call Lee and let her know he would be late because he had a meeting with JR. He explained that he was the attorney for Walt, who Lee knew, but this was more of a personal meeting. Lee had no issue with it, since she knew Greg would never drive after more than a drink or maybe two.

Once settled in at the little corporate bar Greg laid out the story of Corky and his "traveling circus" as he called it. JR was spellbound. Once Greg had brought JR up to date, he continued talking about how he felt about the "legend".

In Greg's words:

*"You know, JR, as Corky's story unfolded some things came into glaring focus for me. You guessed right about one thing. I definitely had to find out why Hilton Head figured so much into the "legend". I mean it came out of the blue for me. Like I told you before, I had only been there once for a business meeting, more of a retreat actually, but never really saw much of the island. I was certainly more pristine than other tourist towns, but I couldn't imagine why it factored so heavily in the story of the young surfer.*

*And then there were this cast of characters. I felt sure each one of them was based on someone I knew or had run across in business. I just couldn't put my finger on who might have been the model for each person in Corky's story. Heck, I didn't even know anyone with red hair, so where in the world did Abby come from? Then there was Duke. I knew a few Duke type guys over the years, the hipster with a heart of gold. Competitive, but charming, a guy's guy. Had your back…that sort of thing.*

*Gabe really threw me. I had been to Hawaii and probably shaken hands with some islanders, but this character was really unique. My best buddy. Never really had a best buddy unless you considered Lee, which I did….and do. Like Lee he was the type of friend you might call "ride or die". All in.*

*Alexa was equally perplexing. I knew in my heart there was a heap of Lee in that character as well. Strong, willful, confident yet feminine at the same time. Not many women could pull that off.*

*I have to tell you my friend, this is all more like a memory than a story. I kid you not. I wonder what that means?"*

JR shook his head and could only muster a "I have no idea, bro…I must say it's mystery. Maybe you have amnesia," he continued only half kidding.

Both men laughed but Greg wondered if there was a grain of truth in that possibility.

After a couple of beers, Greg and JR shook hands and headed home. Greg wondered if they would ever cross paths again. He hoped so.

After talking with JR and then assuming that maybe the final location had been selected, pending Lee's trip there and approval of course, Greg continued to run through the plan in his mind.

Let Greg tell his own story.

That night I lay awake for several hours just going over the plans for the bar. In my mind, I knew exactly the type of beachfront community I wanted to be part of, Hilton Head or not. I envisioned settling in, what the property would look like and even the type food we would serve. Of course, it had to have a surfing theme and I thought maybe I would decorate with black and white pictures of famous surfers riding big waves. I wanted indoor and outdoor seating. Behind the bar I decided a big screen tv showing surf competitions would work since I hoped my clientele would enjoy the work of real artists with the board.

I was a fan of a Virginia Beach based food boat called The Barnacle. At one point I had toyed with the idea of having my bar on a boat but realized pretty quickly that I knew nothing about boating and that the boat would have to be huge.

One thing I knew with certainty was the type of music I'd have on the jukebox. Oh yeah, a jukebox with real records. No piped in music for me. In my mind I heard the Ventures, the Surfaris, Dick Dale and the Deltones and even the Beachboys and Jan and Dean. I knew the last two weren't as legit as the early surf music stars, but most people held them out to be leaders of the surf and hot rod music era. Yep, you had to cater to your clientele. And I had a pretty good idea of who would be attracted to the little oasis. Snowbirds who longed to live the beach bum life, actual surfers who needed a place of their own, local college kids hanging back for spring break who were into the whole nostalgia thing. Yep those were the logical targets.

Maybe I'd even have a little gift shop with souvenir t-shirts, surf music CD's, books on surfing, that sort of thing. Maybe even replicas of CorkBoards™. Of course, I'd have to be careful about the books. Wouldn't want the clientele to become experts at surfing history and who won what. They just had to buy into the vision, the romance and enjoy the vibe. With some help I could make it all happen. I knew I could. I lay awake smiling at the thought.

Up until that sleepless night I hadn't put much thought into a name for the place. I started running ideas through my head. Sandovals, Surfin' Bird, Big Waves, Corktop's. I really didn't like any of them. Finally, I settled on *Corky's Beach Bar*. Just had a nice ring to it. And the logo would be the silhouette of a lone surfer, on the crest of a big wave above the name Corky's. Below that in smaller letters would be the Beach Bar part. But that design could wait for another day. Heck, Lee could even help me design it. Yep…that's the ticket.

The next morning, I approached Lee about taking a weekend trip to Hilton Head. Surprisingly she had no objection at all, presuming we stayed at one of the nice resorts. Ultimately, she picked the Westin at the north end of the island. I wasted no time in getting online and booking an ocean front room starting Friday night. A little pricey to be sure but the web site sold the reason really well.

Next I booked a flight that originated at Norfolk International and got us as far as Savannah/Hilton Head International. We could have flown directly to the island, but Lee had a thing about small planes. We didn't realize at that point that regional jets now served the island. I knew we would need a car, so I also arranged for that online to be picked up at the airport.

Friday finally arrived and we headed to Norfolk to catch our flight. I could see that Lee was excited. I couldn't figure out if the excitement came from our little weekend excursion or the realization that the next phase of our life was about to begin. Didn't matter at all to me as long as my lovely wife was on that plane and by my side.

Off we went on a voyage of discovery.

Of course, when we arrived at the bridge that would transport us to what would potentially be our new home, I noticed that the area was a modern suburban area with lots of shops and restaurants. The little town on the mainland side of the bridge is called Bluffton. I had read it was kind of well-known for its "old town" arts community. I made a mental note to visit there at some point.

Crossing the bridge for me was somewhat cosmic. Damn I hate that word. I'm no hippy (as you might have guessed) but I found the simple crossing of that bridge uplifting in some way that I couldn't put my finger on. I think JR might have been right and that the decision had been made long ago when I first visited the boot shaped island in the Lowcountry.

We checked into the Westin hotel on the north end of the island, dropped our bags and immediately headed down to explore all that the resort had to offer. Lee commented on the lush grounds and the koi pond. First thing I noticed was a cool looking outdoor bar with an ocean view. I convinced Lee to head on over and have a welcome drink. We sat at the bar facing the ocean and soon were greeted by a Jamaican man who identified himself as Duke. Now there's a coincidence.

Duke made us feel right at home and welcomed us to the island in a way only Caribbean people could do. (Authors note: Let me know tell you that Jamaicans know the hospitality business...period. I learned later they have specialized hospitality training on the island. It was clear that Duke was a real pro). I could tell that Lee had let the stress of our business lives in Virginia Beach drain away with her first Tito's martini.

After a while Lee asked, "What's the plan for tomorrow?"

"I think we should just drive around the island getting familiar with all that it has to offer," I replied.

Lee nodded in agreement.

We ended up ordering a few appetizers that would end up being our dinner.

I convinced myself that the next day would define the next phase of our lives. We would soon know.

# Chapter Sixteen

## Is This Home?

I was really surprised when I woke up the next morning and found Lee dressed and ready for our day. She already had coffee in hand and was looking out the wall of windows towards the ocean. I noticed it was very blue today, not always so on the east coast.

"Wake up sleepy head," she said glancing back at me from her fixed gaze on the ocean view.

"How long have you been up?" I asked.

"A good while. Since sunrise in fact."

"Lee, we live near the beach in Virginia. I can't remember you getting up for sunrise up there."

"Then you're forgetting or were asleep," she replied but with no edge to her voice. I even think I heard a little chuckle.

"Anyway, it seems different here. More peaceful or something. I'm eager to see more of the island."

I knew that was a signal to get my butt in gear. I also knew it was a very good sign that she might fall in love with Hilton Head just like I did. I quickly had a shower and we headed out on our little tour. In my mind, if not hers, was the agreeable task of scouting locations for the bar. I didn't realize how many great choices there were and how difficult it would be to make a decision.

Our first order of business was breakfast. Lee believed that it is the most important meal of the day, just like they say. Again, whoever *they* are. We asked the bellman for a recommendation and he said there was a new place mid-island called The French Bakery that everyone was raving about. Lee didn't hesitate to say *"ooh…let's go there"*. Must have sounded classy or she had a craving for crepes. Myself I'm an eggs benedict guy, but "happy wife" and all.

We discovered the French Bakery in a newish open-air shopping area called Shelter Cove Town Center. The center was built on a body of water called Broad Creek and was buzzing with activity. The restaurant offered indoor and outdoor seating, so we decided the day was nice enough to enjoy the outdoors. As expected, Lee ordered something called the "classic French" crepe. Frankly I was a bit confused and after a while made a snap decision to try "Tomasz's Spicy Omelet". I'm not going to waste your time by describing each dish but suffice it to say both were outstanding. We agreed that we would stop back by before we left the island.

Broad Creek looked to be mostly marsh but apparently navigable since we saw a few boats off in the distance. I made a mental note that Corky's might be suited to somewhere on that inland body of water. I imagined how cool it would be for people to be able to boat up to our dock for lunch. Of course, I immediately reminded myself that I had no idea what I was talking…. er..thinking about. That said, I made yet another mental note to find out more.

We spent most of the rest of the day driving from one end of the island to the other. Lee was smart enough to know I was scouting locations and began to take notes. After paying an entry fee at the gate, we spent some time in Sea Pines Plantation but decided South Beach and Harbour Town were well covered with bars and dining establishments. It was a shame too, because South Beach had the funky, rustic feel I knew would work for our purposes.

We checked out Coligny Beach and thought it was too commercial by Hilton Head standards. We visited Palmetto Bay next and decided it had some merit and we would keep it on the list. On the other side of Broad Creek from the French Bakery we came across some nice pieces of land with great views that might work nicely. I fell in love with the view of Palmetto Bay and the large bridge spanning the "creek". That view might win the day.

Later we ended up off of Squire Pope road on a body of water called Skull Creek. Many of the best seafood restaurants were located along that stretch but it provided some interesting possibilities. I just *had* to know where that road got its name and a Google search later at the hotel yielded the origin of the name. Squire William Pope was a wealthy landowner from Hilton Head Island who owned the Coggins Point Plantation. He served in the South Carolina Senate and represented St. Luke's Parrish in the state House of Representatives. Now I knew. Now you know.

We noticed that many neighborhoods, or "plantations" as most were called, were gated like Sea Pines, but you couldn't buy your way in as it was with that huge resort. We agreed that the bar would need to be accessible to all, and that limited our search. None-the-less by the end of the day we had two or three locations in mind. It was about 4 pm when we decided to head back to the hotel. We had spent most of the day in the car and wanted to have a swim before discussing dinner.

There were actually three pools at the Westin, but we selected the one nearest to the outdoor "Splash" bar. After getting wet and swimming a couple of laps we toweled off and headed to the bar for a cocktail. A young lady named Brittany welcomed us and asked if it was our first visit to the island. Lee indicated that it was her first visit.

"I'll bet it won't be your last," the smiling bartender said.

"I think you may be right Brittany," Lee replied.

We stood and chatted for few minutes after ordering some tropical drinks, but things began to get very busy, so we headed back to the pools edge with our drinks.

"So, what do you think?" Lee asked.

"About what?" I said distracted by the magical surroundings, I guess.

"About where you might want to plant your dream bar."

"Well I think it's between Broad Creek or Skull Creek," I said, "Do you have a favorite?"

"To me that's an easy decision. I think it's Skull Creek. There's already both land and water traffic there and it's on a larger body of water," Lee responded.

"Good point. Anyway, I think I'd like to have the bar actually be more or less suspended above the water to improve the view up and down the creek."

"That's going to cost a bundle to build," Lee pointed out.

"Well almost anything you build here will. I just have a vision of how it might look and feel," I continued. "Maybe we can make some enquiries to see if what I have in mind is practical at all."

"Worth gathering more information, I agree."

I was quite surprised at the degree to which Lee had adapted to the idea of opening our own place on this beautiful island. I could see it in her eyes and hear it in her voice. I think I actually had my own island girl. That would be tested in the days and weeks to come but for the time being I decided to relax and revel in the feeling that we shared a dream.

It seemed logical that the next day we would spend speaking to a realtor. We bought a copy of the local paper called the Island Packet and began looking at real estate ads. One in particular caught our eye since the realtor specialized in commercial properties and claimed to have been in business on the island for over 25 years.

We gave Dan Wheeler a call based on that ad and asked if he could meet us somewhere to discuss our goals. I told him we had particular interest in the Skull Creek area, so he suggested we meet at Hudson's. Apparently, Hudson's was almost a historical landmark as restaurants go. Upon our arrival we decided to find seats on the outdoor deck and waited for Dan. He had described himself as mid-fifties with salt and pepper hair. We had to laugh as that described about half of the men on the island.

When he showed up Dan was wearing a Hawaiian shirt and cargo shorts. He walked right up to us as if he knew us even though we had told him nothing about us. Go figure.

"Hi folks, Dan Wheeler," the realtor said offering his hand.

"Hi Dan, I'm Greg and this is my wife Lisa-Michelle."

"Call me Lee, everyone does."

"Well welcome to the island Greg and Lee. How can I help you?"

For the next half hour or so we discussed the sort of business we had in mind. We didn't go into the whole Corky Sandoval story, but did describe the type of structure we saw in our minds eye and the fact that we were creating a surfing theme.

Dan's eyes lit up as we talked about the rustic look and feel we had in mind. Finally, he put up his hand as if to say..." stop".

"I have the perfect property...and luckily it isn't far from here up Skull Creek. Do you want to head up there now?"

It took only about 5 minutes to "head up the creek" as Dan called it and pull into an overgrown parking lot. Dan assured us we shouldn't be too concerned about the state of the grounds and that that view from the property would win us over.

With Dan leading we headed in the direction of the water and finally ended up at the end of a jetty of land with two distinct structures on it. Both looked like they had seen better days. We walked out a dilapidated boardwalk to the first building. Dan began to tell us what turned out to be a pretty sad story.

"Here's the background. Like you, a man named Oglethorpe up from Savannah had a dream to put a first-class seafood restaurant on this property. His problem was he didn't know how to deal with local authorities. He tried for years to get the proper clearances to continue building his dream. Here in the front building he planned a bar with an expansive view of the creek. On forward, where we'll walk in a minute, was supposed to be the main food service area. Again, the selling point would be the views."

"So, what happened?', I asked, kind of dreading the answer.

"He kept fighting town council on this and that and finally ran out of money. He kept a trailer on the property as he developed his plan and after the money ran out, he just sat in the trailer, I guess. Some folks said he drank a lot, but I can't swear to that. Anyway, about a year after he hit bottom he died. A shame too. I met him only once but when he was building his dream, he was the kindest and most enthusiastic human being I think I'd ever met."

Lee and I looked at each other and I saw tears in her eyes. A million things went through my mind at that moment, not the least of which was seeing the original dreamer looking proudly at the half-finished structure imagining what it could be. I ran all the risks and potential rewards through my mind in a split second and then looked back at Lee. All she did was nod "yes".

I looked back at Dan.

"Let's talk money," I said with no hesitation.

We were frankly surprised that the property was priced well below what we anticipated. On the other hand, it was in significant disrepair and we would have to sink a bunch of money into renovations…or even rebuilds. I asked Dan about how much we might expect to pay for contractors and other service people.

"Greg, I'll be honest with you. It depends on the season and how much work they have at any one time. If you catch them at a low point you can make a killer deal. If business is booming out at Palmetto Bluff…good luck."

Dan explained that Palmetto Bluff was an ultra-high-end riverfront community on the mainland. Builders there had big money to spend and attracted contractors easily. He did offer up some recommendations for contractors on the island or "just across the bridge" as he called it. Lee was actually taking notes.

I let Dan know we had serious interest but also told him it was obvious the property had been sitting a while and that any offer we made would be tempered by that fact. He said he completely understood. The bank that owned the property was eager to "dump it" he said, and he would take them any reasonable offer we came up with. Fair enough.

Lee and I headed back to the hotel with a great deal to discuss. Was this going to be our place? Could we afford to make it into something we could be proud of? Was I nuts after all? Once again, time would tell.

# Chapter Seventeen

## Just Do It!

The next three months of our lives were a complete blur. Once we had made our minds up about the rundown property on Skull Creek, we had to retreat to Virginia Beach to close out our lives there. That meant selling our businesses and packing up our personal lives. Nothing would be easy.

I was surprised to find that JR stepped up to help with the selling of the businesses. He did it as a friend, but his legal expertise was a godsend. Using his connections, he quickly introduced me to the owners of a Hampton Roads based CPA firm looking to expand. I found the owners to be reasonable men with a great attitude about customer service. We hit it off immediately. Call me old fashioned, but I didn't want to sell the business to a firm with a fast and loose attitude about customers, or clients as we called them. These guys met my criteria and more. Whew!

After some negotiating, which JR also expertly managed for me, the deal was cut, and we were able to begin visiting my clients to let them know about the transition. Most understood and accepted the situation with resignation if not enthusiasm.

Lee preferred to work with certain of her employees to transition her business to them. Luckily, she had a couple of senior resources who worked closely with her to negotiate a fair deal for everyone.

We ended up with a tidy sum of cash, not enough to completely float the purchase of the property and all the renovations, but a good bit of money none-the-less. I figured we would have to impress a South Carolina bank with our plans and business acumen to acquire the additional funds we needed. Uh huh.

I asked JR to head back down to the island with us to strategize and then negotiate for both the property and the financing. He agreed without hesitation and I was beginning to realize that we might need his services on an ongoing basis. Friend or not, surfer or not, he was a crackerjack attorney and businessman.

It took over a month to negotiate the purchase of the property during which JR flew back and forth from the island to Virginia. We tried to find the final financing even as we worked on the acquisition but that dragged on and on. Lee and I were getting worried that we would end up with a rundown property and not enough money to fix it up.

What happened next was a complete surprise to me. JR was tuned into the Corky story and our dreams, of course, but I never anticipated he would want to be a part of the ongoing saga. One Wednesday evening when we were all having dinner at Reilley's across from our hotel JR told us he'd like to consider becoming an investor.

"Really?" I said, I'm sure showing the surprise that I felt.

"Yep…I've always wanted to do something off the beaten path. Anyway, I came into a bit of money."

"What did you have in mind?" I asked, thinking he would put up maybe a couple of thousand dollars.

"I thought maybe I invest $100,000 in the business and have a ten percent stake," JR said, obviously having given it some thought.

"Come on JR, that would value a business with no track record at a million bucks. That doesn't seem right," I replied wondering why in the world I was trying to talk him out of it.

"Man, you've been watching too much Shark Tank," JR chuckled. "I think this idea has legs and I want to get in early so I can reap the benefits later. Anyway, I know you are stretched at the moment and if I can make a positive impact and help get this off the ground, I feel confident it will pay off. So, think of it this way, I'm a real surfer with real money."

Lee and I looked at each other for what must have been a full minute. Both of us knew that investment would put us over the top and get things moving in a hurry. Again, Lee simply nodded her head.

I turned to JR and stuck out my hand.

"Done!" I said feeling a sense of relief to have a partner with his unique background.

We finished dinner and had a nightcap of Remy Martin to seal the deal.

The next day we completed some paperwork that JR had conveniently already prepared. I should have known.

After that the project picked up steam fast. Just having an attorney on board seemed to impress the lenders. My only hope is that it would also impress the contractors. Dan Wheeler had promised to help us find just the right team if we decided to buy the property and he was a man of his word. He knew a contractor named Marco who specialized in renovations. He was based in nearby Beaufort, so we quickly set up a meeting.

I asked JR to be a part of the initial talks and he suggested that it would protect all parties if we drew up a pretty specific contract. Good news was he was smart enough to build in some late delivery penalties. The contractor balked at first, but my new pal Dan Wheeler twisted his arm just enough to get us a signature. As time went on, I learned it paid to know Dan.

The next order of business was to hook up with a designer who could help with the layout of the bar and restaurant. Again, Dan suggested a lady who had been on the island exactly as long as he had…his wife Ellen. JR thought we should look around a bit, but I saw some of her work and let him know I felt like I owed it to Dan to give Ellen a chance, at least through the drawing stages. Short story, it paid off. Her renderings captured our dream perfectly. She had also worked with the contractor a couple of times, so I felt we had a solid team.

After several days of working on the specifications it occurred to me to ask JR how he was getting by with being on the island for as long as he had been.

"I took some back-vacation time so I could be here to help for a while longer. Anyway, I'm considering moving down and maybe opening my own firm," JR explained.

"How in the world can you afford to do that?" I said knowing it was none of my business.

"Like I said, Greg, I have money".

I took him at his word and on we went. Or "Surf's Up!" as Corky would say.

It took a full six months to complete the structural improvements. We ran into more than a couple of roadblocks, but Marco seemed to be up to the task of overcoming any setbacks and staying on our agreed upon schedule.

Meanwhile, Lee and I worked with Ellen on the interior design. I had told Ellen I wanted to have black and white pictures of surfers in both the bar and restaurant areas. I also envisioned televisions showing surfing competitions and maybe even feature films like "Endless Summer" from time to time. I'd seen that movie at least a dozen times and even in a noisy bar it would play well I thought.

Ellen knew we leaned toward a rustic feel and presented renderings that captured the vibe perfectly. I was surprised and proud to find that Lee provided the most input during that phase. I think her advertising background was already beginning to pay off.

JR pointed out that we wouldn't be in a position to open during peak tourist season that year, but I wasn't particularly concerned. My goal was actually to create a place that locals felt was their own. Not that we wouldn't welcome tourists, I just didn't want our business plan to be dominated by that clientele.

We set our sights on Labor Day weekend for the opening and all agreed that was a realistic goal.

With Ellen and Lee firmly in control of the design I decided to take on the recruiting roll. I wanted to take my time and hire the very best waitstaff, bartenders and cooks I could afford. In the front of the house I wanted big smiles, great attitudes and good humor. I decided that waiters and waitresses and particularly bartenders needed to be performers in their own way. In the back of the house I wanted a head cook who took our bar food to the next level.

I had no idea what I was getting into when I started interviewing. I decided to start with bartenders for the "front room" as we started called it. Since the buildings weren't ready, I decided to interview candidates at a table on the walkway. Worked out well unless it was really sweltering or pouring the rain.

I figured that for the purposes of hiring I had to go ahead and assume the persona of Corky Sandoval. After all the staff needed to buy into the legend so that the customers would too. So, I alerted our team and reminded them to call me Corky if anyone outside the group was around. That got a big laugh out of Marco. Marco laughed big a lot, but he and his crew worked up a storm. I don't really think he caught the subtlety of the request, so I didn't worry too much about him spilling the beans.

My first interview was with a young guy who really looked the part of a surfer. I thought maybe that bit of authenticity might help. I couldn't have imagined how the interview would go.

"So .... welcome to my bar," I said shaking the young guys hand. I noticed he tried to do an odd variation of handshake that I felt like I had encountered back in college, but we finally shook hands in a normal manner. "I'm Corky Sandoval. What's your name?"

"Rock n Roll, Hootchie Koo Purdue, sir," replied the young man shaking his long wavy hair.

"Well that's a unique name…is it real?" I asked.

"Yes sir, signed sealed and delivered at the courthouse, 5 years now."

"Kinda long," I pointed out, "What do I call you….er, Rock?"

"No sir, it's Hooch for short."

"Ha, well that's certainly appropriate for a bartender," I observed.

After a brief discussion, I made a mental note that Hooch was likely a keeper. I was a bit taken aback to find out that he had a degree in Philosophy. Obviously, he was no dummy but as he explained, there wasn't much call for philosophers anymore. So, Jerry Purdue became Hooch…and Hooch became our first employee.

As it had been back at my firm in Virginia, I remembered how much I hated interviewing. I wondered if the candidates could tell.

In any case, the next candidate was equally as interesting as Hooch but maybe not quite so credentialed if you could call it that. Like Hooch, however, he looked every bit the surfer. Again, I suppose I thought that was a real selling point.

"Hi there,", I said, shaking hands with the young man. Again, with the odd handshake. "I appreciate you coming in today. I'm Corky Sandoval, the owner."

"Yes sir, happy to be here and thanks for the opportunity."

"So, what's your name?" I asked, never anticipating another outlandish moniker.

"People call me Peevish McGhee."

"…. ha, ha…is that because you are?" I asked.

'…. uh, are what sir?" the young man said clearly confused by my question.

"You know…. Peevish"

"No sir."

"Then why do they call you that?"

".... well um.... because it's my name."

".... uh.... okay.... Let's move on then," I said realizing that pursuing that line of questioning would simply yield more confusion.

We talked for another half an hour or so during which time I found out Peevish had worked in retail, parked cars in downtown Charleston, housesat for a couple on Tybee Island and in general moved around to find suitable work. At least he had served drinks for a short while at the Tiki Bar on the south end of the island.

I marked Peevish down as a maybe. I found out later after he filled out some forms that his real name was Ronald Peevish McGee. I just had to assume Peevish was a family surname.

The next candidate was an older guy named Wetzell Coker. I figured him to be around 40 years old give or take. In my mind he was a bit James Deanish in his physical presentation, cigarettes in sleeve and so forth. As we talked, I thought he seemed somewhat cynical, but I could tell he was a deep thinker. I didn't ask but he offered up that he was a reformed drinker.

"Do you think it's wise to work in a bar then?" I asked.

"If I understand it, my job is to sell the booze not drink it," he said perceptively, raising one eyebrow. I couldn't disagree.

Like I had done with the other candidates I took some time to layout the plans for Corky's Beach Bar. I was surprised by Wetzell's response.

"It will never work," he said, shrugging his shoulders.

When I asked him why in the world he would say that, his only real answer was *"nobody cares around here."*

My inner voice told me that his put down of the idea immediately disqualified him for the job but in some strange way I liked his cynical attitude. Maybe it would help keep us out of the weeds. Anyway, unlike other candidates he was local and had worked in several bars on the island.

After three days of interviews I had five promising bartenders, a couple of which, including Wetzell, actually knew how to make a credible drink. The next order of business was maybe the most important, hiring a head cook.

# Chapter Eighteen

## The Amazing Juwana Spoon

If I thought I hated interviewing up until now, I really, really hated the next interview. I knew how important it was to have a great cook to oversee food preparation. I couldn't imagine finding or being able to afford an actual chef, of course, but I was hoping I could snag a very experienced short order cook.

And then there was Juwana. Oops…. Ms. Spoon. More on that later.

I had placed an ad in the local Island Packet newspaper describing just what I was looking for in a cook. Juwana Spoon was the only candidate to respond to the ad. Ms. Spoon was a black lady that I surmised was in her fifties with ample girth and a laugh to rival Marco's. She had owned her own restaurant specializing in Gullah cuisine off of nearby Marshland Road, but gentrification had taken the property away from her when she lost her lease.

Maybe I should explain that Gullah, often called Geechee, culture is made up of people who are descendants of African slaves from various ethnic groups. Everyone knows that they were brought to North America and forced to work on the plantations that dotted South Carolina, Georgia, some areas of North Carolina and Florida. Gullah culture has a strong sense of community, history and family. Juwana Spoon was a classic example of the hard working, independent and creative Gullah culture on Hilton Head Island.

Interviewing Juwana Spoon got off to a rough start.

"Well Juwana, thanks for coming by today. I'm Corky Sandoval, the owner of this new restaurant," I started off.

"Please Mistuh Corky, call me Ms. Spoon."

I found myself saying "yes ma'am".

I explained that I needed someone to run food service totally since neither Lee nor I had any background in that particular art.

"When do I start Mistuh Corky?" Ms. Spoon asked taking a lot for granted.

"Well I thought I might ask you a few questions first.... uh...Ms. Spoon."

"No need, I'm your choice Mistuh Corky, no one else do what I do...ax'um anyone on de island."

"Do you have any references?" I asked hopefully.

"I jus told you Mistuh Corky...ax'um anyone on the island, anyone, eb'ryone."

I have to say I had no particular reason to doubt anything this lady was telling me. In fact, I hired her that minute and did "ax'um" around later. Several islanders including Dan and Ellen not only backed up her claims but indicated we were very lucky to get her. Made me feel kind of smart or at a least a better judge of people than I had given myself credit for. Or maybe I was just intimidated.

We were roughly a month and a half away from our grand opening but I was worried about losing Ms. Spoon, so I put her on salary right away. We agreed that we could use that time to do menu planning and vendor selection. We would also need to hold interviews for waitstaff and lower level cooks as Labor Day drew near.

I also went ahead and hired Wetzell, Peevish and Hooch with the agreement that they would work around the site until the opening on the holiday. Wetzell had done some construction work and ended up helping Marco. Marco didn't mind at all since he was bound and determined to come in on time and on budget. I let Peevish and Hooch start working on the drink menu knowing full well I'd need to review it once completed.

The front building or bar area was far enough along that we were able to set up makeshift work area so that Ms. Spoon and I could kick around ideas for menu items. Late one afternoon I came to the table with several items I was proud of, the kind of pub grub that drew crowds I thought.

"So, here's what I have in mind Ms. Spoon," I said and began rattling off what I thought were cool selections to go with the island lager that was bound to flow.

I had my "Buc-an-ear Menu" ...ten varieties of corn on the cob... always one dollar.

Corn dogs...also one dollar each (I imagined them dipped in Dijon mustard. Yum)

Wings ...5 varieties...one dollar each.

Peel and eat shrimp – lots of flavors…. buck a cup, that's about five shrimp (I figured you couldn't charge a buck each!)

Buck a burger – sliders really.

BaBBQ – buck a barbeque slider…. small cup of slaw no charge.

When I was finished with my little presentation, I was beaming but Ms. Spoon looked at me like I was from outer space.

"Mistuh Corky, you de buckruh ta be sure. But you worry about de bar snacks and Ma'am Spoon worry 'bout de food."

And that was the end of that meeting. Ms. Spoon later told me, but only after I asked, that in buckruh she was referring to me as the owner. I chuckled to myself later when I looked it up and found out it had lots of meanings really. Plantation owner, white man…nothing derisive necessarily used in the context she used the term, but it more or less put me in my place.

I did need to push back on our new chef (and oh yes, she insisted she was a chef) in that her menu tended toward Gullah. But she soon agreed and broadened the selections to include seafood and other more traditional American dishes to be served in the front building or the actual restaurant. I was feeling like this talented lady and I were forming a workable team and I didn't even mind being called "buckruh Corky" once in a while.

Ms. Spoon handled finding all of our food vendors, making deals with local fishermen and other seafood providers, butchers and so forth. I noted that she was very particular about baked goods. After all, sandwiches would be a big part of our offerings as well as dinner rolls and even pastries.

One afternoon she came to me and said, "I'm gwine down to de sprout store for some *real* bread and cake. Dat stuff."

I came to find out she meant a local bakery called Sprout Momma. Apparently, the baked goods there, including the breads she would use to make our sandwiches, were the talk of the island. It was run by a mother and son team, Kim Tavino and Ryan Fennessey who both had an interest in great tasting food that was also healthy. After that visit she wouldn't allow us to buy from any other supplier and Lee wouldn't serve any other breads at home.

I have to admit that I was beginning to relax as far as how the menu was being designed and managed. Ms. Spoon obviously had a lot of experience and know how. More important perhaps was a work ethic that made all of us work harder.

I still managed to get my "Buck an ear" menu adopted, but only in the bar section and only if I used freshly made to order Sprout Momma buns for the sliders. Fair enough.

# Chapter Nineteen

## The Home Stretch Approaches

Now that we had a rough idea of our various menus and had a basic staff in place, I was able to turn my attention to some of the things Lee and Ellen had been working on. Ellen was delivering on my vision of a rustic yet comfortable bar and grill with an obvious surfing theme. She was able to find the television monitors I wanted for each section and work with a content provider to have surfing features looping at all times.

The turf around the structures tended to be kind of rough. We made a decision to try to approximate a beach as you approached the bar. It took several truckloads of white sand but eventually we had fashioned a fairly credible beach. Ellen bought some Adirondack chairs and placed them strategically. Her thought was that if there was a wait to be seated, folks would be able to relax on our makeshift beach. I really hoped we had that problem.

Next order of business were the black and white pictures I had always planned for the walls. That little detail had gone back to my early dreams of having my own place. Out of necessity the surfers in the pictures had to be anonymous so that some might reasonably be taken for "me" back in my championship surfing days.

Ellen had all of the necessary contacts to hook us up with a photographer out of southern California who had a massive catalog of prints. Some were already in black and white and some could be printed that way on demand. Ellen provided me with a link to his web site and I spent most of two days picking the prints I thought best suited our needs. Luckily, we could simply order the prints and have them framed by a local shop.

One photo really caught my eye. It was of a man coming out of a huge barrel looking intent and graceful. The photo was labeled "Gentle Ben at Half Moon Bay". Ben? My mind was clearly playing tricks on me, but I decided I had to have that print.

After my review we put a list together of the prints we wanted, and Ellen contacted the photographer directly to place the order. After completing the call, she found me at my makeshift desk in the front building.

"Boy that was strange," Ellen said looking perplexed.

"What do you mean?"

"I told the photographer I was working on a place called Corky's Beach Bar owned by Corky Sandoval and he said, 'oh yes…I've heard of him.'

"Just a mistake I guess, or he was trying to impress you," I suggested.

"I don't know, he said he knew you had won a bunch of championships 'back in the day'. It's just a bit spooky."

"Well maybe it's a good sign. We want Corky to be real to our customers too. It's a start," I said laughing.

"Weird," Ellen said again. Should I mention the Gentle Ben coincidence, and weird her out even more?

The pictures were delivered ten days later and by that time the place was looking pretty darned good. Ellen took the photos over to the framing shop. She had warned them we wanted a quick turnaround since grand opening was less than a month away now.

Ms. Spoon had continued interviewing and now had a team of four additional cooks, two to work during the lunch period and two for the dinner service. While some of the finger food could be prepared in the bar itself, the main kitchen in the restaurant could also provide more involved dishes as needed. It was only a short walk between the buildings.

I have to say Wetzell Coker had become an integral member of our team. It seemed like he had his hand in everything. He made some suggestions on how the bar was laid out, for instance, and even had the courage to advise Ms. Spoon on one of her dishes. Of course, she blew off his advice, but he lived to tell the story.

Given Wetzell's now more enthusiastic involvement I asked him to help with the final interviews for servers and let him know he would supervise them and the bartenders. He was surprised but gladly accepted the challenge. I think his cynicism was beginning to fade…or at least it seemed so.

The next day Lee had a huge surprise for me. The UPS truck brought two large packages. Inside were longboards. Even though I already knew it I was happy to see that she really understood what it would take to promote the bar. The boards seemed to have been well used. I hugged her and ran my hand over one of the boards. I felt stupid because at first, I didn't notice the logo at the end of the middle stripe.

CorkBoards™!!

My wife had yet again proven why she was my hero.

We decided to install the longboards on the walls at both ends of the bar. We figured it would promote some conversation about Corky's adventures. Being basically a capitalist, I found myself wondering about protecting that brand. I don't know why I didn't think of it before, but I called JR and asked him to handle registering it. He did a trademark search that same day and said it should be no problem.

I decided to take a chance with the brand and asked Lee to create a t-shirt design. After only a day or so she came back with the silhouette of four surfers, two male and two female, apparently riding the same wave with the name CorkBoards ™ in script below the image. At that moment the brand was officially born. I had no idea yet what we might do with it other than sell t-shirts, but maybe there was money to be made.

Ellen was excited to tell me the framed photos would be available within a week and we could begin placing them. I decided the Gentle Ben photo belonged right above the bar. I also decided not to tell anyone ever the real name of the surfer. I decided it was me. Corky. Me.

One feature that I was happy Ellen selected for the bar area was a jukebox that functioned two ways. If left unattended it would play a constant stream of whatever type of music you selected. Or you could interrupt the stream and select a song from the flippers that suited your mood. If you don't know what I mean by flippers you're a millennial. Nothing wrong with that. Just sayin.

Let me give you an idea of my thinking about the appropriate music for Corky's. First let me tell you that I actually met Jimmy Buffet. I kind of knew that might be the first artist that popped into your mind. When I met him, it wasn't at a concert or after party or anything sexy. It was at a symposium on management of musical artists for CPA firms.... boring! He was quite friendly and mixed in well with us guys in suits. More power to him. He is the CEO of an empire...but to me his music, while clearly beach music of sorts, isn't surf music unless you count the song "Surfin in a Hurricane". Sorry Jimmy.

To me surf music was and is Dick Dale and the Deltones, the Surfaris and maybe Jan and Dean and the Beachboys. In fact, I guess, surf music IS the Beachboys....not the Tams and Chairman of the Board etc.....the Myrtle Beach scene. And I say that knowing that only Dennis Wilson ever actually surfed.

Ellen arranged for a stream that included traditional surf music and just enough Buffet to satisfy the masses. But the flippers featured my selections. Good mix I thought.

It was coming together nicely but we thought we had better have a meeting of the entire critical team to map out plans for the grand opening which was scheduled for a Saturday night in two weeks. I asked Ellen, Lee, Ms. Spoon, JR and Wetzell to meet with me in the now mostly complete bar area. Hooch and Peevish were milling around and I gather listening in but not part of the main meeting.

Ms. Spoon started off by running through the menu for the main restaurant. She had planned a few special items for opening night including a poached lobster concoction that frankly went way over my head. On the other hand, Ellen and Lee swooned at the thought.

Ms. Spoon did of course have to offer up at least one Gullah selection just for that night. She took a full ten minutes describing a Gullah/Geechee stew she planned to brew all day for presentation that evening. *Just the ticket when it's 95 degrees out* I thought to myself but knew better than to object.

I let Wetzell go over the pub grub. Far less intriguing to be sure but even Ellen and Lee agreed the selections were interesting. Ms. Spoon of course only managed a "mmm…. mmm…. mmm".

After finishing the review of pub grub Wetzell brought up the idea of entertainment for the night.

"I really think we should put on the dog and have a really hot band play for grand opening," Wetzell said.

"Um…. put on the dog?" I said laughing out loud.

"So, I'm old…so what?" Wetzell replied smiling but again raising that eyebrow. "No seriously, I know this band called Sweet Doggy Dugan and the Big Wave Surfers out of Florida that can draw a crowd wherever they play on the island or actually anywhere in the southeast. I think we should see if they are available."

Something told me Wetzell had already lined them up since a band that in demand would almost certainly have a gig for a Saturday night in two weeks.

With that in mind I found myself saying, "Okay Wetzell, make it happen."

I think I saw a sigh of relief. After all, if we hadn't agreed to hire them, he might have had to pay for them himself. But in the end, he was right and anyway Dan had already told me they were the biggest surf band around. In fact, back in the 60s they had a big surf hit called "Barrel Roll". These guys had to be at least my age but in any case, I was glad Wetzell had taken action.

And speaking of Dan he had walked up just about that time, presumably to pick Ellen up. That was my cue to make my little speech.

"Folks, I want to tell you how much I appreciate your hard work in making this little dream of ours come true. It's been something like forty years in the making, one way or another. Without each of you Lee and I couldn't have pulled this off. And JR I want to especially thank you for your work up in Virginia and down here. You came out of nowhere to take us across the finish line and I'll always be indebted."

The group erupted into applause and JR held up a hand to silence them.

"Guys, JR is another world. Here I'm Joey."

Everyone clapped again. I knew JR didn't use the name Joey often and wondered about the transition. Boy did that ring a bell. Anyway, on to grand opening!!

Surfs up!

# Chapter Twenty

## Late Night at the Tiki Bar (Never tell Corky he can't do it)

"Aw heck, I know there's no appreciable surf here. You're lucky if you can get a wave big enough to body surf into the beach. But there are a lot of surfer wannbes hanging around the ocean front. Some are just kids but a lot of them end up on the island later in life, full of bravado and their own "semi true stories' about big waves and beautiful wahinis…. sure guys… it'll work. And hey, stop by for a drink and trade stories. You'll see. Glad to have you."

# Chapter Twenty-One

## Grand Opening

I have to admit…for the first time in my life I was panic stricken. It hadn't happened when we left Chicago and our former life and livelihood behind. It hadn't happened when we did that very same thing and left Virginia Beach. Why now?

As I told our team, the dream of opening this waterfront bar was over forty years old. I had a group of really smart people working with and for me. None- the-less, when opening night arrived, I was almost catatonic.

In the past few days I had realized that everything was on the line. At my age I had no realistic way to start all over again. This was it. All the marbles. And it scared the bejesus out of me. After all, what did I know about running a beach bar? What did I know about food service?

Luckily my lifelong rock of a wife picked that very night to reassure me that she was in my corner. In fact, she surprised me by saying some words I didn't think I would ever hear.

"You know what, Greg, I think this little cruise has become my fantasy too," Lee gazed out over Skull Creek and back towards our creation…. Corky's Beach Bar.

"I have to admit I had my doubts," she continued, "But by golly you pulled it off."

Somehow that vote of confidence immediately corrected all my misgivings. Come hell or high water (heaven forbid a storm surge) we were going to make a go of this.

It was 5:30pm and having been refreshed by my wife's calming words I began walking around the bar area checking with each employee to insure we were ready for the 7pm kickoff. I knew Juwana Spoon would have the restaurant area running like a clock, so I didn't worry so much about that part of the business.

In fifteen minutes or so Sweet Doggy showed up with his band and entourage. By entourage I mean a group of "old hippies" as Lee called them, all of whom seemed to have some job associated with the rock and roll menagerie.

Sweet Doggy was a very tall, rangy guy with grey hair pulled back into a ponytail. He had a big expansive smile and when he shook my hand, he totally enveloped it.

"Yo, Corky, long time no see," Sweet Doggy said inexplicably.

"Sorry, man, have we met?" I said having no idea how that could be the case.

"Well I expect you don't remember but it was back in Virginia Beach, must have been …I don't know…68, 69. I was playing at a place on the pier".

For a moment I just stood there. Sure, I had lived in Virginia Beach…but not in 68 or 69. I should have immediately said something like *"you must have me mistaken for someone else,"* but I didn't. I could have said, *"maybe you are confusing me with Corky Carroll"* …but, I'm sure you know, I didn't. I could have said a lot of things but instead I just said:

"I have a vague recollection, but anyway it's an honor to have you with us for this opening night. I always loved your music."

In reality I had no knowledge of anything, but his one sixties hit, and that was only because Wetzell sat me down at the bar and played the tune on our very special jukebox. The song was all twangy guitars and vocals processed through heavy reverb. Definitely not the Beachboys but catchy enough.

"Well surf music built me and my lady a house but you real surfers made it all possible," Sweet Doggy said. As usual I winced but stayed silent.

We had had a local entertainment contractor build a respectable stage out on the sand and made sure we had plenty of power cabled out so that band could plug in whatever devices they needed. Marco, our main contractor for the structure, insisted on supervising. I have no idea if he had any concept of what he was doing but he had taken responsibility for insuring things got done correctly and I just decided to trust his judgement. He pulled it off with his usual big laugh. Somehow, like my wife's comments, that just made me feel a bit better.

The windows in the bar area could be opened towards the makeshift beach and therefor the stage and we brought in several Adirondack chairs for patrons to enjoy while The Big Wave Surfers were playing. It took some doing to get Beaufort County to allow us to serve drinks out on "Corky's Beach," as we all called it, but JR...excuse me...Joey posted a surety bond of some sort and it was done. I would rather have an attorney working for me than against me...that's for sure. Particularly one that surfs.

The plan was to have a ribbon cutting of sorts at 7o'clock on the walkway that lead from the parking lot and beach to the bar structure. I had told the team I would say a few words and planned to stick to that "few words" promise. Shortly thereafter Sweet Doggy said he would lead off his set with Surfin Surfari. Somehow, I just knew that was the perfect kickoff song.

As I walked up to the makeshift ribbon, I looked around me to see Lee, Joey, Juwana (I mean Ms. Spoon of course), Ellen, Dan, Wetzell, Hooch and Peevish and a few others all standing in a sort of semicircle. Every one of them seemed to be beaming. I knew all of my team had a sense of pride that we had pulled off this improbable feat. I was proud of all of them. Really very proud.

I was really glad that the local paper, the Island Packet, had decided to send a reporter and photographer. That had to be good.

Out on the beach I could see Mark, Aimee, Brittany, Ryan, Kim, Duke, Taline, Beth and Sara. All of our island buddies who were there to wish us good luck with our venture. That felt good.

When 7pm rolled around I took a wireless mike from Wetzell and started to offer my welcome. "Started" is the operative word. I immediately began to tear up as the words I was trying to say stuck in my throat.

Finally.

"Friends, countrymen, islanders…lend me your ear," I said. There was a robust laugh from the crowd that seemed to number in the hundreds at that moment. I have no idea of the actual count.

"This evening has been a long time in coming. Lee and I have worked our entire lives to create a place where we can all get together and talk about how surfing has become a part of island life and, in fact, life in so many places in the United States. Heck I know we don't have "big surf" here.... but we do have The Big Wave Surfers" here to make this a special evening. On behalf of the Corky's Beach Bar team...thank you so much for being here!"

At that moment and before I knew what was happening Lee, who had been standing beside me the entire time, grabbed the microphone and said."

"Let's have a big round of applause for our big kahuna, my husband, .... Corky Sandoval!"

I looked at her and then back to the crowd and waved as The Big Wave Surfers launched into Surfin Surfari. No music had ever seemed more appropriate or sounded sweeter.

I only wish Gabe, Duke and Abby were here to enjoy the moment.

# Chapter Twenty-Two

## The Legend Continues

After three months of summer business Lee and I were quietly celebrating the success of Corky's Beach Bar. The locals had adopted our little venue and the Island Packet newspaper had spread the word about the "new kids in town". I couldn't have been more pleased.

Juwana turned out to be a sensation. She had even earned an article in CH2, a rather hip magazine for and about the island. Of course, little was made of our restaurant but, then, Ms. Spoon was an icon and any good publicity for her was good publicity for us.

Wetzell Coker was, in fact, a dynamo in terms of running the bar. His cynical attitude had turned around completely and he embraced the surfer bar as if it was his own. That really helped relieve the day to day stress.

You'd think with servers named Hooch and Peevish you'd need to keep an eye on the cash register but that wasn't the case at all. Our team seemed to take the success of the venture very seriously and, in fact, money was rolling in.

As for me, I thought that the best place for me to help grow the business was behind the bar. After all, the surfing champion everyone expected needed to be front and center.

One evening I was serving drinks to what turned out to be a nearly full house when a gentleman my age found a seat at the bar. Like Sweet Doggy he had long hair, although it was only salt and pepper as they say. It was also pulled back in a ponytail. He was dressed in a t-shirt with a San Diego logo on it and cutoff jeans. I hadn't seen anyone wear cutoff jeans since college but maybe I've led a sheltered life.

Given that we were what appeared to be close to the same age we struck up a conversation. I guess you would say it meandered from surf music to weather in the lowcountry (you do remember what I'm referring to don't you?) to politics. I enjoyed the conversation and we found a fair number of similarities in our lives.

We talked for well over two hours that first night and I found that I felt a kinship with this guy. He told me he had done some surfing when he was younger but had given it up because of a bad leg.

Over the next several days my new friend showed up fairly regularly and each time we were able to have a rousing conversation, mainly about the music and exciting times in the sixties. I came to know him as Barry. He didn't mention his last name and I didn't want to push it. Who knows, he might be a fugitive or something. I guess he would tell me when he felt more comfortable.

I think over time Barry became my prototype customer and I found myself telling him about Corky's, that is my adventures surfing on the east coast. I told him about Abby, Kaapo and everyone else in the troop. Sometimes he laughed out loud but mostly he just nodded knowingly. I guess he must have lived a similar life.

Sometimes Barry would say the most profound things like, "I'll bet Abby loved that!" He seemed to have really latched on to the cast of characters, which surprised me, but I must admit made me pretty happy. The stories had legs. That was my goal all along.

Oddly Barry really didn't tell me too much about his life, but I thought that was likely because something in his past caused him some pain. I decided his story would come out one day as our friendship grew.

Late one Wednesday afternoon in the spring Barry and I were chatting as usual and I was in story telling mode (I guess one day I'll write that novel I keep thinking about). Since Barry seemed receptive to those tall tales and semi true stories, I offered up another one.

"Hey Barry, did I ever tell you about my adventures in the Caribbean?"

"No, Corky," Barry chuckled," Do tell."

And I did.

**The End (for now)**

**Sweet Doggy Dugan and the Big Wave Surfers**
**Album called "Barrel Roll" (first released in 1965)**

### Side One
Barrell Roll
Who Put the Shrimp in the Cheese Ball (Joey's song)
Grom No More
Pipeline of Your Love
Dog Trax in My Surf Wax
Goofy Foot, Goofy Mind

### Side Two
Surfer Curl
Throwdown on Wrightsville Beach
Bored with My Board
Hippie Surf Stomp
I Gotta Woodie (how bout you?)
15 Feet and Rising
Nose Ride
Barrel Roll (extended version)

## Sneak Peek at "Corky's Caribbean Adventure" coming soon

When Gabe, Abby and I left Half Moon Bay headed for points east I had planned on returning to Cali within one year, maybe a year and a half. After all I was born there and that's what felt like home. Sure, I went to school in Hawaii and loved surfing there, but the west coast was in my blood.

So here I am sitting with Gabe on the boardwalk in Daytona Beach, Florida two years later and he's trying to convince me to head for the Caribbean. As usual he had done some homework and found that there were several spots with a decent surf break and even a few competitions that might work for our group. Duke had mentioned visiting the Virgin Islands one day over lunch and that set Gabe off.

After that lunch with Duke I also did a bit of research on surfing in the Caribbean and pointed out to Gabe and Duke that in Jamaica the islanders didn't even use a proper surfboard. Sometimes they "rode the waves" as they called it with little more than an old door.

"So much the better," Gabe argued, "Maybe we can sell them a few boards during our visit."

I'd have to say that things more or less spiraled out of control in the next few days. Gabe managed to get Abby, Alexa and Stacy on board. As usual, Skipper didn't object so technically I was outvoted. A trip to the Caribbean islands was in order. The next step was figuring out how our crew would get there.

I guess I had to meet with Andy and Roger. I think our new plans would come as a surprise to both of them.

The adventure continues (I think)

Printed in the United States
By Bookmasters